M000029334

An Evil

~Inspired by a story many claim to be true~

By
Thomas Brittendahl

Copyright © 2016 Thomas Brittendahl
All rights reserved.
ISBN: 978-0692633533

TABLE OF CONTENTS

AKNOWLEDGEMENTS

I would like to thank the support and patience of my parents, without whom I would not have been able to dedicate as much time to writing. Thank you also to SolaFide Publishing for putting on the SYWTBP contest, and for their support for independent writers of all genres.

CHAPTER ONE

The Bellomy Family

Paul Bellomy knew something was wrong when he woke in bed, sweating, as if he'd just had a nightmare he couldn't remember. James . . . it had to be James . . . *again.*

Paul sat up, looked over his wife, to the clock on the nightstand: 5:20 a.m. Sarah was still asleep on the far side of the king-size bed, her back to him, light brown hair draped over her bare shoulder, the covers tucked soundly under her arm.

Paul rubbed his face, certain his eldest son was at it again. His feet met his slippers on the ground, his eyes peering outside. The cool wind danced with the tall redwoods as the last of the moon's light gleamed off the calm waters of the small lake. Next to his wife's beautiful face and the smiles of his eight children, the view from the glass double doors leading out to the second story balcony was his favorite view. "God is good," he mumbled softly, reminding himself of his fortune, despite his son's phase in skepticism.

James. He needed to check on James.

Stepping lightly, he walked from his bedroom, then down the hall. James' door was closed. Paul softly gripped the handle, turned quietly, then opened the door slowly. He huffed a frustrated breath, gritted his teeth, then closed the door with a soft *thump*.

On his way back to the master bedroom to get his cellphone, Paul remembered Rebecca, his eldest daughter. She was supposed to be home last night from her friend's house, but Paul had gone to bed before she got home. Once at her room, he opened the door with less care than before. "Christ Almighty," he mumbled when she too was still absent.

His gut tightened as he went room by room, checking on his remaining children, making sure they were in bed. They all were, except Jacob, his eighteen year old.

Paul rubbed his hand through his brown hair as he walked back to his bedroom, grabbed his phone, then walked downstairs to the kitchen. James was the first he called, but only got voicemail. He tried Rebecca, but got the same. Finally he tried Jacob, but his luck fared no better. Looking up to the heavens with his soft blue eyes, he took a deep breath, prayed for his children's safety, and his own patience for when they finally got home. He then sent each a text.

An hour passed with no reply from any of them.

Paul waited for his children's reply in the back yard, watching the sun peak its way over the distant mountains. The compact, two story guest cottage fifty-yards away was supposed to be a transition for his older children, a way to get them used to being on their own while still not too far from home. However, the more they stayed out all hours of the night, the more Paul was determined to keep them under *his* roof. He feared for his children, not only that they'd return safely, but that they weren't going too far down the path of sin. James was twenty-two, in college, and developed the unpleasant habit of spewing Hume, Nietzsche, and other heretical thinkers around the house. Rebecca was twenty, went to the same college, but as of yet hadn't developed any of James' habits. Paul regretted not sending them to Trinity.

When seven o'clock came and went, Paul started making changes to his sermon. He was the evangelical leader and head pastor of Riverwood Church, the church he founded sixteen years ago. Last night he was all set to talk about charity, but the more time passed the more he worried about all the sinful influences in the world, and how his children could remain devout in such a secular age.

At seven-thirty, Sarah came out back, wondered what he was doing. He told his wife about their children, then asked her what they should do. "Trust in God," she said smiling, her beautiful green eyes still melting his heart. She held a mug of coffee, took a sip, added, "We need to love God, too, just like He's loved us."

That was it! She'd just given him his sermon.

"Come on inside, sweetheart," Sarah said, walking back towards the open double doors that led to the kitchen and family room. "Come on, get yourself some coffee."

At ten o'clock on the dot, Paul stood on stage, dressed in his fine dark blue suit with a deep red tie, brown hair parted to the right, blue eyes peering out over the crowd of ten-thousand. The love for his parishioners was near that for his family, who sat in the front row, all but his three eldest, who still hadn't replied to any of his messages.

Fifteen minutes into his sermon, Paul needed to wipe his forehead with a small towel before continuing. "I earlier borrowed words from our dear friend, Mr. Jonathan Edwards, who graced the earth with his presence three hundred years ago, because he put it much better than I can. Like in his time, we are facing a crisis of faith. We are living in a land so corrupted by ungodly people, so immoral and twisted by the deception of evil, that the idea of right and wrong has lost its meaning."

Paul paused for effect.

"How are we to know *the right* from *the wrong, the good* from *the bad*?" Paul asked, looking over the crowd, listening as they shouted out answers. Most he heard answered correctly. "That's right." He smiled holding up his favorite book. "The Bible. The truths offered in these stories offer us the key to understanding the right from the wrong. It gives us the key that will ensure our salvation and everlasting life with God."

Paul paused again, took a moment to give a special smile to his wife and children. He saw the pride in

Sarah's green eyes as she looked back to him, then to their children.

"All we must do is *love God*," he continued, looking out over the crowd. "That's right, we must truly and unconditionally love God. Belief is not enough. Belief in something only acknowledges its existence." Paul walked to the other end of the stage. "Any man can believe in anything. How many of you believe in evil?" Paul looked out upon the hands. "It looks like not *all* of you believe in evil," he said laughing. "I believe in evil. I believe in Satan. I believe that Satan not only exists, but is the source of *all* evil. However, do I love him? Do I love the source of evil?"

The audience shook their head, answering for Paul.

"That's right my friends, the answer is *no*. I accept that Satan exists, but I reserve my love for God, the enemy of evil, the enemy of Satan. God is good!" Paul exclaimed over a cheering crowd. "If God is good, then He must be incapable of evil! For me, that makes loving God rather easy, doesn't it? Which is good, because if the Bible makes one thing clear it is that we must love God. Deuteronomy 6:5 tells us to 'Love the LORD your God with all your heart and with all your soul and with all your strength.' John 3:16 says, 'For God so loved the world, that he gave his only Son, that whoever believes in him should not perish but have eternal life.'"

Paul paused and stared for effect.

"Believing in Jesus is to believe in His teachings, His words. In John 14:15, Jesus says: 'If you love me, keep my commandments.' Might we actually have the answer from Jesus Himself on which commandment, of more than six-hundred, is most important? In fact, we do! Matthew, Mark and Luke all tell us the same thing; they tell us what Jesus answered when He was asked what commandment is the greatest: 'Thou shalt love the Lord thy God with all thy heart, and with all thy soul, and with all thy mind.' The testaments do not contradict on this fact."

"We love God," yelled a man from the crowd.

"Good," congratulated Paul, "because that is the test, that is all you need to do. God loves those who love Him, God lets loose those who do not. If you give your unconditional love to God, He will pull you through even the most dark and troubling times. If you trust in the Bible, you cannot go wrong."

Paul again paused for a few seconds to let the cheering crowd express their joy.

"So, my friends, the question becomes, which would you rather be: loved, or abandoned?"

"Loved!" rejoiced the crowd.

"Then show your love for God, let him hear your praise," implored Paul to the cheers of the crowd. "Let everyone hear your love, your praise for the Lord our God!"

The crowd erupted and the music was cued. It was another perfect sermon.

Paul mingled after the service with those who wished to meet him. He always made himself available for any question or comment. Most people just took the opportunity to tell him how much he meant to them, how his books helped pull them through troubled times. He always made a point to be the most polite person in the room, and always tried to accept their praise with the humblest of hearts. Loretta Coleman gushed with praise as a few members of Paul's family approached.

"Oh, Mrs. Coleman," interrupted Paul, standing outside the auditorium-chapel in one of the entrance and exit halls. "I don't mean to interrupt, but I would like you to meet my wife, my sons Adam and Bryan, and my daughters Samantha, Julie and Katy."

"Aren't they just precious," gushed Loretta. "How old are you little darlings?"

They all answered with smiles on their youthful faces. Katy was eight, Julie was ten, Adam was twelve, Bryan was fourteen, and Samantha was sixteen, each one born about two years apart, just as Paul and Sarah planned.

"Oh, aren't they just precious," repeated Loretta. "And it is quite a pleasure meeting you, Mrs. Bellomy."

"Please, call me Sarah."

"I hope I get the chance to meet the rest of your children someday," Loretta said.

"Yes, unfortunately, the other heathens couldn't make it today," regretted Sarah with a joking smile on her face. "But, they should be here next week."

"Oh, let's hope so," Loretta said, her brushed on eyebrows raised. "We wouldn't want them to become atheists now."

"Certainly not . . . but we have faith God knows what's best for them," Paul said laughing, but then prayed silently just to help his children along.

Soon, all the parishioners left and Paul drove his family home. The kids wanted to stop off and get some ice cream, but Sarah told them they had plenty at home. When Paul turned on the radio, the whole family began singing the tune. "He's got the rivers and the mountains, in His hands; He's got the oceans and the seas, in His hands; He's got you and me, in His hands; He's got the whole world in His hands . . ."

As they pulled off the main road, through the security gate, up the six-hundred foot gravel driveway on the way to their seven bedroom estate, Paul and Sarah stared at each other and thanked God for all they had.

The moment they walked through the front door, Paul went upstairs to his room and again tried to call his children. He dialed James first.

"Hello," answered a scratchy, tired voice.

"James? Where are you?"

"Hey dad . . .. We're on our way home . . . . We should be there in a few minutes."

"Where are you? And who's *we*? Is Jacob with you?"

"We're—" The phone went dead.

"James . . . James . . . are you there? Damn it!" Paul tried redialing, but the phone went to voicemail after a few rings. "Damn it!" He tried calling Jacob, but the call went to voicemail right away. He left another message to call, then tried his daughter. The phone rang once, then he heard the ringer in the house. Rebecca didn't answer, but Paul followed the sound down the hall to Rebecca's bedroom. He opened the door to her lying in her bed asleep. "Jesus, Mary and Joseph," he yelled out, waking her up. "You nearly gave me a heart attack young lady. Where've you been? I tried calling you like ten times!"

"I'm sorry, dad," Rebecca said, covering her face with a pillow, "but my cell lost service at Jill's house."

"You were supposed to be home last night!"

"I meant to call you, but my phone lost reception up there."

"Did their landline lose reception too?" There was no answer. "You're grounded!"

"Dad! That isn't fair—I'm twenty years old!"

"So long as you live under *my* roof, you will abide by *my* rules."

Rebecca raised her arms up to the ceiling, made two fists, then slammed then down onto her comforter. Paul was just about to say something else, but just then saw out the window James' car making its way up the driveway. "We'll talk more later," Paul said, then closed her door, ran down the stairs and headed outside to lash out at his other disobedient children. "Where've you two been?" Paul asked as his two eldest sons stumbled lethargically out of the car. "Your mother and I've been worried sick about you, not to mention you missed church . . . again!"

"It's my fault dad," James said, raising his hand.

"Are you drunk? Are you both drunk?"

"I'm just tired. He's hungover," James said with a chuckle before rubbing the scruff on his face. "Last night he was drunk."

"Thanks a lot," Jacob said, snapping a betrayed look to his elder brother. "You said—"

"Go to your room and don't come out until I say so," Paul said sharply to Jacob, who held his stomach as he slowly made his way to the house. "You wait a minute," Paul said as he turned to James. "You know better—what were you thinking?"

"I was looking out for him."

"By getting him drunk? I don't care if you have a drink now and then, but Jacob only just turned eighteen, he's not even out of high school yet, and you're already getting him drunk?"

"Maybe if you'd lay off him a little he might not feel the need to hide things from you; maybe he wouldn't try to wait out a hangover."

"Don't you talk to me in that tone, young man. 'Children, obey your parents in everything, for this pleases the Lord', Colossians 3:20."

"'Fathers, do not provoke your children, lest they become discouraged,' Colossians 3:21," replied James. "I can read just as well as you, *dad*."

"You go inside, and do *not* let me see you until dinner," Paul ordered angrily and with his finger pointed towards James. "If you wish to continue this behavior you can move yourself right on out of this house, and not to the cottage!"

"Good! I don't want the damn cottage anyway. Just give me a week or two and I'll be out of your hair."

"Go to your room!"

"I'm going!"

Paul followed James into the house. Before making his way up to his room, however, James stopped by the kitchen to get a tall glass of water and a few pieces of bread.

"Go to your room!" Paul yelled.

"I'm going!" James yelled right back.

In the family room, Sarah sat with the other children watching television, all twelve eyes looking at him instead of the screen. Paul took a deep breath, prayed for God to watch over his son, then joined his wife and the rest of his children in the family room.

Hours later when it was time for dinner, the children began piling around the table. The sun was almost completely behind the mountains, but the last of the day's light gleamed off the lake. Paul remembered the moonlight from the early morning, then thanked God He'd kept his children safe.

"You're always hungry," teased Sarah as Adam was anxious to dig in.

"I'm a growing boy," replied Adam.

Paul laughed at such a cute remark from his son. "You are indeed. Will someone get James, Rebecca and Jacob, please?"

"I will!" volunteered little Katy.

"I'll go with you," Julie said, then ran off with Katy through the kitchen, under the arch to the foyer, then up the stairs.

"Don't you eat yet," Sarah reprimanded Adam and Bryan as she smacked their hands. "Samantha, make sure your brothers mind their manners."

"Yes, mom," replied Samantha, who then stuck her tongue out at her younger brothers.

Paul saw, but only chuckled under his breath. Jacob and Rebecca made their way to the table, Jacob looking very hungry. "How do you feel, Jacob?"

"Terrible."

"Do you plan on doing such things again?"

"No, father."

Katy and Julie ran back to the table, Julie raising her arms in victory for beating her younger sister. "It's not a race, darlings," Paul said as the whole family was at the table, except James. "Girls, did you tell James?"

The two little ones nodded. Just then, James could be heard slowly making his way down the stairs, each footstep banging harder than the previous. When he came around the corner his wavy brown hair was messy and he looked like he just woke up.

"That is what the night is for, son," Paul said with a smile.

James didn't reply to his father. "The food looks great," he remarked to Sarah.

Paul did not like being ignored by his children. "James, why don't you lead us in saying grace today."

James stared at his father for a few seconds. "You know what dad, today I think I'd rather not."

From the corner of his eye, Paul noticed his children's eyes snap his way. "Do you wish to eat, son?" Paul asked calmly.

James huffed a loud breath. "I do."

Paul smiled. "Then you'll lead us in grace."

The two stared at each other, neither blinking an eye. Finally, James broke off, stood from the table. "Forget it, I'm actually not very hungry."

"Where are you going?" asked Sarah.

"To my room."

"I don't think so, son," disagreed Paul. "You will sit at this table regardless of whether you eat."

James laughed under his breath, but retook his seat.

"Jacob, why don't you lead us in grace," requested Paul.

Jacob obliged. "Which one?"

"Whichever you want," replied Paul.

Everyone put their hands together and bowed their heads.

"God, we give you thanks from our grateful hearts for this meal, for our fellowship, for your love, for your provision of food and of those who prepared this wonderful meal for us. Help us to remember that you are with us around the table and may our hearts and words be a blessing to you in return. Amen."

"Amen," replied all except James.

The family dug in. When James reached for a piece of meat, however, Paul snapped. "What do you think you're doing?"

James raised an eyebrow. "I'm eating."

Paul slowly wiped his mouth with a napkin. "Now, son, I'm confused. Just a moment ago you said you weren't hungry."

"If I need to sit here, then I may as well eat."

Paul nodded. "I see. Well, as a member of this family you are most certainly welcome at this table." James continued to reach for the meat. "However," Paul interrupted. "I asked you to say grace. After you say grace, you may help yourself."

"What if I think grace is stupid?"

The other children all raised their eyebrows. Paul was about to snap, but caught himself before he lashed out in front of the entire family. Instead, he laughed. "How can it be silly to give thanks to God for all the blessings He's bestowed upon this family? Come now, son, I know it's been a rough day, but after you say grace, you may help yourself to all the food you can eat."

James huffed another loud breath. "Fine. Which one?"

"Like with Jacob, which one is up to you."

"Come Lord Jesus, our guest to be, and bless these gifts bestowed by Thee."

"Amen," finished Paul.

"Amen," repeated James with a role of the eyes.

Paul saw it, but thought it better to ignore the gesture. "There. That wasn't so hard, now was it?"

James glared back for just a moment before mumbling, "No."

Paul nodded. "Good. Now, you can eat."

James didn't speak for the rest of dinner. He sat quietly as the others talked. Paul saw that he was acting defiantly, but, so long as he didn't spoil the mood for everyone else, Paul let him stew in his own misery. He knew they'd talk later.

A few hours after dinner Paul found himself sitting out on his back yard porch, gazing up at the stars. He saw the face of God in the bright lights above and wondered at the majesty of it all: how something so marvelous could be viewed by him always filled his mind with questions. The questions always ended with a humbling admission, an acknowledgment that if he could answer them, he would have to be God; and since he is not God, there was no point struggling to find an answer.

Sarah peaked her head over the balcony of the master bedroom. "Honey, what are you doing out there?"

"Just enjoying the stars."

"Are you coming up soon?"

"I'll be up in a few minutes."

Paul sat a few moments longer before heading up to bed. On his way through the kitchen he saw James and Rebecca watching television in the family room.

"Turn that down a little, will you . . .. Thank you. Goodnight."

"Goodnight dad," Rebecca said, not turning her head from the television.

Paul kept waiting for James, but a reply never came. "Good night, James."

"Night," is all James gave.

Paul laughed a little under his breath. He would let it go for the night. "I love you guys," he said, then continued on.

"Love you too, dad," Rebecca said as he left the kitchen.

James sat silently.

Paul made his way up the stairs, stopped by all his children's bedrooms and looked upon them in bed. When he came to Jacob, who went to bed right after dinner, he remembered getting drunk in his own youth; remembered sneaking out of the house with a small bottle of his father's liquor to share with his friends. He smiled and continued on to his room, confident that Jacob was simply about to go through a phase he went through himself; and one within which his eldest child found himself. Before he got to the master bedroom he saw Samantha praying by her bedside. Paul smiled, then thanked God for all his blessings.

"I saw Samantha saying her bedtime prayers," Paul said entering the master bedroom. "Did the other kids say their prayers before they went to sleep?"

"I'm not sure about Jacob," Sarah said. "But, the others did—I had to help Katy with hers—she was so cute."

Paul nodded. "I suppose I should say mine now, too."

Sarah got out of bed and joined Paul by the bedside.

"And now I lay me down to sleep, I pray the Lord my soul to keep, Thy angels watch me through the night, And keep me safe till morning light. Teach me to always say what's true, Be willing in each task I do, Help me to be good each day, And lead me in thy holy way. I pray whatever wrongs I've done, You forgive me every one, Be near me when I wake again, And bless all those I love, Amen."

Paul laughed as he and Sarah slowly got to their feet. "I tell you, it sure used to be easier to pop right up."

"Maybe next time you should include a line for stronger bones," joked Sarah as they got nestled into bed next to each other. The bed was warm. Sarah reached over and turned off her light. Paul decided to sit up and read a little of his Bible. "Did you talk to James at all while you were down there?"

"No. I could tell he was in no mood to talk."

"Maybe you should just let him move into the guest cottage? It would mean a lot to him."

Paul grumbled.

"You will talk with him tomorrow, right?" Sarah asked, gently placing her finger tips on Paul's forearm. "I hate it when you two go to bed angry with each other."

Paul took his wife's hand, brought it to his lips. "Yes, I'll talk to him tomorrow. A good night sleep will serve him well."

"I just hate to see him move out on such terms."

"He'll be fine. All young adults go through moments like this. Rebecca seems to have begun her rough patch, and Jacobs' seems to be right around the corner."

"It scares me, Paul."

"I know. It scares me too. But, so long as we have faith, we can count on God's good grace to continue blessing this family. The more we love God, the more he'll love us in return."

"Amen," said Sarah.

Paul continued reading, but his mind began to wander. "You looked amazing in church today. I'd be lying if I said I didn't get distracted every time I set my eyes upon you."

"Really. Well, I'd also be lying if I said that I'm sorry for distracting you."

Paul smiled as Sarah unbuttoned her nightgown, then slowly slid it off. Her naked body was warm and soft. They made love as passionately as when they first got married. The gentle thrusts slowly got faster, and harder. Paul's hands slid up and down her body; hers gripped his back. As Paul looked into his wife's eyes while making love to her, he was reminded of all the goodness that existed in the world.

CHAPTER TWO

Evil Approaching

"He's got the whooollle world, in His hands; He's got the whole wide world, in His hand; He's got the whooollle world, in His hands; He's got the whole world in His hands . . ."

Paul slowly opened his eyes.

"Good afternoon listeners, you are listening to 99.1 KLTS, the area's all-day Christian rock station. It's time for today's verse of the day: first Peter, chapter five, verse eight says, 'Be sober-minded; be watchful. Your adversary the devil prowls around like a roaring lion, seeking someone to devour.' Today's verse is brought to you by the Riverwood Evangelical Church . . ."

Paul checked the clock—2:47 P.M. He sprung to his feet, breaths heavy, the master bedroom spinning in circles. His head throbbed and he felt nauseous. He just made it to the toilet before the vomit reached his mouth.

"What is going on?" he mumbled aloud as he flushed the toilet.

He took a few moments after expelling last night's dinner to regain his bearings. The first thing he noticed was his damp clothes. Then, he noticed his body felt drained of all energy—his joints and muscles tightened like he'd been in a fight all morning. He couldn't remember a time when he felt so terrible. He laid out on the bathroom floor just before passing out.

The slow breath of life. One breath after another, Paul regained consciousness. The bathroom had stopped spinning. His nausea passed, but his body was still sore and his head still pounded. Slowly, he made his way to his feet. When he finally gained his balance, after using the sink for support, he exited the bathroom and sat on the end of his bed. He looked to the clock: 3:07.

"What happened?" Paul asked as he put his hands to his head and almost passed out again. He felt his pant pocket vibrate. "Why am I dressed? Why am I wet?" He pulled the phone from his pocket, shocked to see over thirty new messages and even more missed calls. "What happened?"

Paul began checking his messages. About half were voice-mails and the other half text messages. The texts were mostly his wife wondering where he was. The next most were from his literary agent, Stan, who tried to get ahold of him to go over the upcoming book tour. Paul sent a message to his wife telling her that he was alright, but that he couldn't talk at the moment. She responded asking if he still planned to pick up the children from school.

Paul made his way downstairs and downed a tall glass of water before opening the fridge and scarfing some of last night's leftovers. He then chugged one more tall glass of water. When he went for his keys, they weren't in the bowl at the end of the countertop. "Where the heck are they?" he asked as he began looking all over. Finally, he saw them on the floor next to the front door. They looked like they had been randomly thrown or dropped at the spot. After picking them up, he headed to his car.

Once in the garage, he scratched his head. "Where's my car?"

After going back inside he was further perplexed when he looked out the window and saw his SUV sitting outside on the drive way in the rain. "No. I parked it in the garage yesterday." It was forecasted to be a sunny and warm day, but outside it was wet, cold and dark.

Paul sent out a mass message to every member of his family who had a cell phone: "Are you alright?" read the text.

Sarah quickly responded, returning the question to her husband. Paul told her that they would talk later and that he was on his way to pick up the kids. He got in his car and headed to the various schools.

While on his way to pick up Adam, Julie and Katy, Paul received a message from Samantha saying that she and Jacob were fine and waiting for his arrival. Then, Bryan responded saying the same. When Paul pulled up along the curb of the elementary school, he saw his three youngest waiting patiently for him. "Hey guys," he said with a smile. "I'm sorry I'm late."

"That's okay daddy," replied Julie. "We knew you were going to be late."

Paul smiled. "How did you know that baby?"

Katy whispered to Julie not to tell. "Katy's friend told her," Julie replied.

Katy's eyebrows lowered and lips shot out into a huge frown. "You said you wouldn't tell."

"But dad asked me a question."

"Girls, girls, that's enough. Katy, which friend told you?"

Katy shook her head. "I was told not to tell, daddy."

"Katy," snapped Paul, glaring at his daughter. "Tell me who told you that I was going to be late."

"My friend doesn't have a name."

"Katy," Paul said again. "Daddy asked you a question." He looked to Adam and Julie, both of whom shook their heads and shrugged their shoulders. Katy sat with her head down, her pouty lip sticking out. "Katy, sweetheart, it's very important that you tell me who told you."

Katy began crying.

"Katy, darling, tell daddy who told you."

"Rachel," said Katy.

"Katy, how did Rachel know daddy was going to be late?"

Katy continued crying. She shook her head and said she didn't know.

"Okay . . . okay. Daddy will call Rachel's parents later."

Paul continued on to pick up Bryan from the junior high school and then Samantha and Jacob from their high school. On the way home, Paul stopped off at the gas station when he saw his low fuel light come on.

"I had a quarter of a tank yesterday when I got home," he mumbled.

When Paul pulled into the station he told his children to stay in the car.

"I'm going to go in and buy a candy," Jacob said.

"With what money?"

"I found two dollars at school today."

Paul looked at his son, disbelieving his claim, but not caring enough at the moment to challenge it. "Just make sure you get something you can share with your brothers and sisters. Acts 20:35, 'it is more blessed to give that to receive.'"

Jacob rolled his eyes but did not argue.

Paul got out and swiped his credit card into the pump. While the machine was processing, he opened his gas tank and took the nozzle from its holder. Paul rolled his eyes at the time the machine took to process the needed information. Finally, the machine rendered its verdict. However, for Paul, the verdict was a rejection of his credit card.

"What is this now?"

He swiped his card again and waited for the machine to accept his card. After a short time, the same verdict was returned. Paul tried a different method. He swiped his ATM card and entered his security code. Unfortunately, the machine indicated that his card was declined. Paul angrily removed the nozzle from his gas tank. He overheard Katy singing in the car without any music since the radio was off, "He's got the whole world, in His hands . . ."

"God, give me the strength," prayed Paul.

He went inside the gas station to talk to the attendant. As he approached the door Jacob made his way out. "Remember, share that with your brothers and sisters."

"I will," promised Jacob.

Paul swung the door open and greeted Larry, the owner of the station. "How goes it today, Larry?"

"Hey there, Paul," Larry replied, "I have a full load of cars to repair—so, for me at least, things are going well."

"I'm happy to hear that." Paul threw his cards on the counter. "The darn machine out there rejected my cards."

"Well, that doesn't make sense."

"No, Larry, it doesn't."

"Here, let me try it in here."

"Thanks, just put forty on two."

Larry took the credit card and gave it a swipe. "Hmm," Larry said shaking his head. "That's funny—it came back declined."

Paul took a deep breath. "Very well, let's try the ATM."

"You got it." They went through the same routine with the same result. "Why, hell, your card's been declined."

"Are your machines working properly?"

"I haven't had a complaint all day."

Paul nodded. "Larry, can I ask a favor of you—"

"Don't even worry about it, I know you're good for it."

"Thanks Larry."

Paul went out and pumped his needed gas. As he stood at the pump he felt his phone vibrate. "Hi, honey."

"Paul, we have a problem," Sarah said.

"What now?"

"I'm at the bank and they told me that we have no money."

"What?"

"They told me you came by earlier and closed all our accounts."

Paul's stomach churned in frustration. "Just, stay there. I'll drop the kids off and head right over." The nozzle clicked as he hung up. "God, give me the strength," he prayed again as he got in the car and headed home. He gave a friendly wave to Larry as he exited the station.

When Paul drove up to the house, past the tall trees that lined the driveway and were gently blowing in the wind, he noticed the front door to the house was wide open. No cars were in the driveway. Paul stopped in front of the porch and ordered his children to remain in the car.

"Jacob, make sure that none of your brothers and sisters get out of this car until I come back out through the front door—do you understand?"

"Yes, father."

Paul slowly exited the car and approached the front door. He froze when the door closed about half way. The wind made sounds like moans and screams as it passed through the many trees on their property. Just as he mustered the courage to continue, the door flung back. He again stopped in his tracks.

"Dad, be careful," yelled Samantha from the car.

Paul glanced at his children's faces, all looking on in fear. He put up his hand telling them that everything would be alright, then walked to the door. It again closed about half way, right before the wind rushed through and pushed it fully open. *The wind . . . it's just the wind.*

Once Paul stood in the doorway, his hand started shaking. "Hello! Is someone in here?"

No answer. The sound of the rain falling made it difficult to listen to the sounds in the house. Paul again put his hand up to his children, trying to calm them as he closed the front door so he could better hear.

"Hello!"

Slight sounds could be heard on the second floor—like someone rummaging through belongings. Paul grabbed the first defensive looking object he could find—an umbrella. He then slowly made his way up the stairs.

"Deliver me, O Lord, from evil men . . ." Psalms 140:1-5 was the first prayer that popped into his head, so Paul kept repeating the passage as he drew closer to the top. The rummaging grew louder with every footstep. When the staircase creaked, the rummaging stopped. Paul stood still. After the rummaging sound resumed, Paul too followed suit, slowly making his way to the second floor. "Guard me, O Lord, from the hands of the wicked; preserve me from violent men, who have planned to trip up my feet."

Paul made his way down the hall. The sound came from his bedroom. The master closet was slammed shut and drawers were now being gone through. Paul prepared himself to engage his enemy. Paul placed his hand on the door knob and prepared himself for the worst. Then, as Paul froze, the sound of footsteps made their way to the door.

I'm caught!

Gritting his teeth, Paul opened the door and, without even looking, raised the umbrella high above his head and yelled at the top of his lungs.

Rebecca screamed even louder.

"SON OF A—" Paul stopped himself. "What in God's name are you doing in here."

Rebecca turned off her ipod and took out her earphones.

"Jesus Christ dad! You nearly gave me a heart attack!"

Paul immediately went up and hugged his daughter who had jumped back onto the bed. "I'm sorry . . . I'm sorry . . . I thought you were an intruder."

Rebecca began laughing. "Why would you think that?"

"Why did you leave the front door wide open?"

"I didn't know that I did."

"Well, what the heck are you doing with our bedroom door closed; and what are you doing going through your mother's clothes?"

"I needed to use the mirrors on the back of your doors. Jill dropped me off because mom said I could pick out and wear one of her dresses for my date this Friday."

"Your what?" Just as Rebecca started to answer, Paul cut her off. "Wait here a minute." Paul ran downstairs and opened the front door. With a big smile he waved his children in the house. Rebecca followed her father downstairs. "Rebecca, for scaring the daylights out of me, I want you to stay here until I get back—help Jacob babysit."

"But, dad, Jill is going to be back any minute."

"Then, she can help too. Why didn't you take your car? Where is your car?"

"I—"

"Never mind. I need to go—I should be back soon— we'll talk about this date of yours when I return."

The children ran into the house.

"We thought you were a bad guy," Adam said, giving the evil eye to his sister.

"Or a ghost," added Bryan.

"Start your homework," lectured Paul before heading out to the car.

As he reengaged the engine he saw little Katy standing in the doorway waving goodbye. Paul waved back as he circled around and headed for the gate. "Crazy kids," Paul mumbled with a laugh, thinking of Rebecca.

Paul began driving away when he looked in his rearview mirror and saw Katy still standing in the doorway waving goodbye. However, when he looked closer, he noticed a dark shadow standing beside her, holding her hand as she waved with the other. Paul slammed on the brakes and the car screeched to a stop. Frantically, he turned and looked again. Katy was still waiving, but there was no shadowy figure besides her. Paul's blood was boiling, his mind confused. "What the hell is going on?" Paul put the car in reverse and quickly backed up to the house. "Katy, was their someone by you just now?"

Katy shook her head. She smiled at her father and, without saying a word, closed the front door. Paul closed his eyes and took a deep breath. "Lord, give me the strength, keep me from losing my mind."

Just then his phone rang. It was Sarah.

When Paul finally got to the bank he saw Sarah sitting on a chair looking frustrated and confused. "What took you so long?" she asked.

"Oh, the rain, and the kids . . ... What's going on here?"

"I think you better talk to the manager."

The two sat patiently as the bank's manager finished with another client. Sarah's face looked grave, her expression of disbelief concerned Paul.

"Hello, Mr. Bellomy," greeted Ted, the bank's manager. "Come to redeposit that money with us?"

"What are you talking about, Ted? Why does my wife tell me that we have no money in our accounts?"

"Because, sir, you came by earlier and closed them all out. Why don't we go over to my desk."

Paul and Sarah followed Ted to his corner office. Ted took a seat and invited them to do the same. He stared at Paul and Sarah for a few moments before Paul asked, "What happened to our money, Ted?"

"Mr. Bellomy, I told you: you came by earlier and closed all your accounts—we have your signature; we have your thumbprint; we have a video. I was surprised myself, I tried my best to persuade you to stay with us, but you were adamant."

Paul shook his head. "No . . . no . . ... This doesn't make sense. I want to see the documents; I want to see the video."

Ted nodded and rose from his desk. He welcomed them to help themselves to any of the candies on his desk while he retrieved the documents.

"What did you do?" Sarah asked.

Paul turned to his wife, surprised that she would think him guilty of such an act. "I didn't do anything. You wait and see—there will be a problem somewhere in here. That, or someone is messing with us—some kind of fraud."

Sarah raised an eyebrow. "I hope so."

It took about five minutes before Ted returned with the documents. "Is this your signature, Mr. Bellomy?"

"It looks like it," agreed both Paul and Sarah.

"I would ask you if this is your thumbprint, but who really can tell such a thing," Ted said with a laugh. "I can always have this verified, though."

"Do that," demanded Paul.

"Very well. It will take some time, though."

"Just do it," demanded Sarah.

"You said you had me on video?" questioned Paul. "Where is the video?"

"This is most unusual, Mr. Bellomy. But, if you will follow me, I will let you see yourself on camera."

Paul and Sarah followed Ted to the security room. Ted ordered the video be played of Paul's earlier transaction. Paul and Sarah looked on in disbelief.

"Are you going to deny that's you, Mr. Bellomy?" asked Ted.

Paul looked at himself, first in line, then talking to the teller, then Ted showing up and taking Paul to his desk. The camera followed Paul's every move. Paul looked at his clothes, which were the same he wore in the video.

Sarah put her hand over her mouth—Paul watched in horror. He and Sarah were speechless.

"Are you satisfied?" asked Ted.

Neither Paul nor Sarah answered—they just stared at the monitor.

"If you feel now that you made a mistake," continued Ted, "we can always just put everything back to normal."

Paul and Sarah turned to Ted—a faint look of hope showed on both their faces.

"Just return the check and we can make everything how it was," informed Ted.

"What check?" asked Paul.

"The cashier's check," said Ted, "the one made out for over forty-million dollars."

"Yes," said Paul, "the check—if the account was closed, then you would have issued me a check."

Ted smiled. "That's right, and I did—if you have it, we can create a new account and get you back to normal."

Paul stood petrified.

"Do you have it?" asked Ted.

"I don't know."

"What do you mean, you don't know?" Sarah asked, nearly to tears.

Paul went flush and gripped his hair with his hands. "I don't know," he repeated, gritting his teeth as he uttered the words.

"Did you take it to Straight Talk yet?" asked Ted.

"Straight Talk?" questioned Paul.

"Yea, the web-based, non-profit, progressive research and information center," clarified Ted.

"Yes, I know who they are," Paul snapped.

"Frankly, I was shocked when you wanted the check issued to them," added Ted.

"Why would I have you write the check out to them?" yelled Paul.

"I don't know, Mr. Bellomy, but, please, calm down. I simply did what I was told to do, even after trying to persuade you from doing so. But, it was your money."

Paul breathed heavily, said a silent prayer.

"You might want to make a stop by Straight Talk and see if they still have it."

"Can't you put a stop payment on it?" asked Sarah.

"No, I'm sorry, Mrs. Bellomy, but it's a cashier's check."

It took Paul and Sarah a while before they could get themselves to leave the bank. Paul already went into the bank drained, but he left looking even more pale. Paul begged Sarah to go home while he made the trip to Straight Talk, but she demanded to join him.

It took about ten minutes to get downtown and to the Straight Talk building. When they arrived, they went straight in and asked the receptionist if she had seen Paul earlier in the day.

"Yes, sir," answered the young lady. "The place has been a buzz since you left."

"Did I drop anything off when I stopped by?" Paul asked.

The young lady smiled. "Yes, sir, you did. You put a check on my desk for forty-million—"

"Mr. and Mrs. Bellomy, welcome to Straight Talk," interrupted and greeted Mark Masterson, one of the chief editors. "Although we were completely shocked, we were also most gracious for your donation earlier today."

"Our what?" snapped Sarah.

Paul held back his wife.

"What else would you call it?" Mark asked, smiling through his thick mustache.

"A mistake," replied Paul. "Can we please just have the check back, then we'll be out of your hair."

"You can't have it back, Mr. Bellomy, we've already cashed it," informed Mark.

"You snake," yelled Sarah.

Paul, again, stepped between his wife and the editor.

"Look, Mark, we've had quite a bit of history between us, and I know that most of it is not friendly, but whatever happened earlier today was a mistake. I am asking you to please, just give me back my money."

"No," Mark said sharply. "We can use that money, put it to good use."

"Mark, I'm begging you." Paul got down on his knees and took Mark's hand. "Please, Mark, think of my children—you know I have eight children. Whatever hatred you feel towards me, don't let that affect my children. Please . . . please . . . for the love of God, give me back what is rightfully mine."

Mark smiled. "I find it ironic that you would get on your knees and beg me to return the money that was freely given by you." He laughed. "Perhaps you can pray to your god—a god that doesn't exist—maybe he can grow you some more."

Paul snapped, leaping to his feet and punching Mark in the mouth. After falling down Mark yelled for security. "You fucked up, pal. I was going to cut you a break and give you back a small portion, but now I'm not going to give you shit. I guess you'll just have to crawl back to that church of yours and ask for more donations."

Paul went livid. He and Sarah resisted the security.

"You evil, evil, man," scorned Sarah.

"You'll pay for this, Mark," Paul yelled. "As God is my witness, you *will* pay for this!"

CHAPTER THREE

Evil Acting

James turned off the road for home and slowly made his way up the long gravel driveway. It was almost nine, and already the swaying trees gleamed under the light of the full moon. The wind had been strong all day, but the rain had died down since night had settled in.

"God dammit," James mumbled when after about one-hundred feet he looked in his rearview mirror and saw the gate failed to close. "The god dammed sensor must be acting up again." He put the car in park, got out, and started walking towards the gate.

BOOM!

An explosion of thunder went off, just as a very strong burst of wind moaned and screeched. James jumped back, lost his balance, and fell to the ground. His heart pounded as he looked around. After a few moments of panic, he began laughing at his silly mind. "I thought for a moment something was there," he said as he made his way to his feet. "Stupid fear, stupid supernatural nonsense."

Only about thirty yards from the gate, James continued on with a smile on his face, but his hands still shook. He shook them out, then slapped his jeans to get the small pebbles off.

"Alright," James said approaching the gate, "let's get you closed."

Gripping the lower metal beam, he pushed hard, forcing the gate closed and manually latching it so it did not reopen.

James stood for a moment looking down the dark road, lit only by the bright moon. Street lights could be seen about five-hundred yards down the way, but on their little stretch of pavement, no street lights were ever installed. He was about to turn around and head back when he glanced a strange figure standing in the distance. "What the hell?" Shielding the wind with his hands, he squinted to get a better look at the figure. "Is that . . . a person?"

The figure was about one-hundred yards away. It looked like the outline of a man, but with the body of a shadow, one with depth. It stood in front of a large pile of salt and pepper granite boulders and seemed to make subtle movements. A soft moan came from the distance, from the same direction as the dark, shadowy figure. The longer James stood still, the louder the moan got, and it seemed to get even closer. It was as if the shadow stared straight at him.

A rush of adrenalin forced James to turn and run for his car. As he ran, he felt like he was being followed.

After about fifty feet he turned and saw the shadow standing just outside the gate. His heart sunk—the figure was still staring. Turning again to run, the moans grew louder, like they surrounded him. Screeches could be heard inside the moans, like either cries for help or calls to flee.

When James got to his car the gate slammed open and the wind again knocked him to the ground. The moans and screeches overtook him, and it was again like a thunder drumming in his ear. When James looked back, the shadow had not progressed—it remained standing just off the property. Scrambling to his feet, James hopped in the car, started it, and peeled out down the driveway, finally stopping only to run to the front door.

When he got to the front door, James looked around one last time. The figure was gone. The wind was as strong as ever, but the shadow had disappeared. The gate swayed back and forth in the distance, but there was no way he'd venture back out to fix it.

After safely making it inside, James peeked one last time towards the gate before closing and locking the door. His head resting over the peep hole, he took a moment to take a few deep, soothing breaths. After gaining his bearings, James again laughed at his silliness before letting his body slide down the door till his butt rested on the hardwood floor.

Rebecca came out from the kitchen. "What are you laughing about?"

"Nothing," James replied after another a deep breath. "So, I heard you pissed dad off yesterday, too?"

Rebecca smiled. "It's not hard to do."

"What did you do?"

Rebecca looked over her shoulder before answering. "I stayed over at Jill's house."

"Jill's hot."

"You don't have a shot. She's with Vince, he's one gorgeous guy—he goes to State too."

"Was he there the other night?"

Rebecca nodded.

"Were there other boys there last night?"

Rebecca nodded again.

"Does dad know?"

Rebecca shook her head.

James laughed.

"You won't tell, will you?"

James shook his head. "Of course not."

"Jill was here earlier, you know, you just missed her."

"Well, sucks for me." James picked himself up and walked into the kitchen. All his siblings but Bryan and Adam were either watching television or doing homework. "Where's mom and dad?"

Rebecca shrugged her shoulders. "Dad said he'd be back soon, but that was like six hours ago."

"Where's Bryan and Adam?"

"Upstairs somewhere, probably in their room."

James nodded, then walked over to the table where Samantha, Katy and Julie sat. Katy and Julie were drawing, and Samantha looked like she was struggling with some homework. "Is that geometry?" James asked.

Samantha nodded, her light brown curly hair falling over her face. "I don't get this one."

James took a look, mumbled the problem out loud. "True or false: the contraposition of a statement has the same truth value as the original? Okay, well, let's try an example, shall we?" Samantha nodded. "If a given polygon is a triangle, then it has exactly three sides, right?" Samantha squinted, looked to the ceiling, then nodded. "Okay then, if a polygon has more or less than three sides, then it's not a triangle, right?"

Samantha closed her eyes, moved her lips like she was reciting something, then opened them. "So, it's true?"

"You tell me, kiddo."

Samantha nodded.

"Okay, then, check the back of your book for the answer."

Samantha did, then pumped her fist. "Ah ha! I was right!"

"Nerd!" little Julie blurted out, then continued drawing.

Samantha shook her head back and forth singing "Shake it off."

"You shouldn't have told on me earlier," Katy said.

Julie breathed loudly. "I had to, I couldn't lie to dad."

Katy glared, then continued drawing.

James chuckled, looked over to Julie's and Katy's drawings. Julie's was a simple drawing of all ten members of the family lined up in a row from oldest to youngest. Katy's was odd, no color, just a dark form, like what he'd seen outside. "What is that, Katy?"

"My friend."

James raised an eyebrow. "Do you see your friend?"

Katy shook her head. "Not right now."

"Katy—" James was about to ask if Katy spoke with her friend, but Jacob walked up to him and punched him softly on the shoulder, then gestured him to follow outside.

"Thanks for yesterday, by the way," Jacob said when they stood alone on the back porch.

"I told you not to worry, right? I knew I'd take the worst of it."

Jacob chuckled. "I still feel a little sick."

"It'll pass. Keep drinking water, or just have another beer. Don't laugh, it'll help."

Jacob shook his head. "I'd rather throw up."

"You already did plenty of that the other night."

Jacob nodded. "Thanks again."

"No worries. Next time, though, when you and your friends feel like having a few drinks, make sure you have a house you can drink at—I don't want to get another call to pick you up again from a park."

Jacob nodded again. "Okay."

"Hey, if you do wind up at the park again, don't hesitate to call."

Jacob smiled, nodded, then led them back inside. Julie was nearly to tears. "Stop! You're so annoying! Stop!"

"Whoa, whoa, whoa . . . what's the matter here?" James asked.

Julie looked her cute little eyes up to him. "She won't stop singing."

As Julie spoke, Katy continued singing softly, almost in a whisper, "He's got the whooollle world, in His hands, He's got the whole wide world, in his hand . . ."

"She's not singing loud, I can barely hear her," James said. "The t.v.'s louder than she is, and that's not bothering you."

Katy turned to Julie, stuck her tongue out.

Samantha looked up. "Will you two just knock it off," she said, then looked to James. "They've been going at it like this ever since they got home."

James shook his head, then looked to the television as Rebecca stopped flipping the channels when their parents' names flashed on screen.

"We are reporting on a strange story that we got word of earlier," reported the local news. "It seems that evangelical leader and bestselling author, Paul Bellomy, senior pastor of the local Riverwood Church, showed up here, to the Straight Talk headquarters downtown, and donated over forty-million dollars to their organization."

Photos of Paul and Sarah were put on the screen.

"Later," continued the reporter, "the pastor and his wife returned asking for the donation back. Apparently, when the recipients of the original donation refused to return the money, things got a little out of control."

The station showed a video of Sarah and Paul losing control of their emotions after refused their money. Their mother was seen lunging at a man and their father was heard cursing the same man.

"The cops were eventually called to the scene and took the Bellomy's into custody," the reporter continued, "but just a little bit ago the evangelical couple left the police station, where it seems no official charges have been filed."

"What the hell?" James said, shaking his head. "There's gotta be a mistake. Dad wouldn't give a dime to Straight Talk—he probably wouldn't take money from them either."

Jacob snatched the remote from Rebecca and changed the channel. "Give it back you little brat!"

"Turn it back, Jacob, I want to see what's going on," James insisted.

The second Jacob raised his arm to switch back the channel, the garage door opened and headlights lit up the foyer. All James' siblings stopped what they were doing, their eyes looking back and forth to each other. A few seconds later their parents staggered into the house, long faced as if someone had died.

"Hi mommy, hi daddy," Julie said from the kitchen table.

It was as if their father didn't hear Julie; his head stayed down as he went straight for the stairs. "Hey baby doll," Sarah said walking into the kitchen, her tone tired as she dropped the keys off on the counter. She looked up to each of her children, then started crying.

"Mom!" James said approaching. "Mom, what happened?" he asked as he put his hand on her back, but she kept crying into her hands. "We saw the news . . .. Is everything alright?"

She cried even harder. "I don't know," she said, then turned and hugged him.

All the other children huddled around their mother, all except Katy, who remained at the table, drawing, singing softly to herself, "He's got the whole, world, in His hands . . .."

Sarah took a few loud breaths before speaking. "I'm fine, children. I'll be fine, your father will be fine . . .. We'll all be just fine."

She didn't believe it, James saw the fear in her green eyes. He'd never seen her so terrified. "Mom—"

"James, please help put Julie and Katy to bed, tonight." James nodded as his mother looked to Jacob and Samantha. "Don't go to bed too late you two, don't forget you still have school tomorrow." Sarah then looked over all her children. "I love you all very much . . . we'll talk more tomorrow, okay?"

Each child nodded. "I love you mommy," Julie said, followed by the rest.

James walked his mother up the stairs, then told Adam and Bryan they'd talk tomorrow when they asked Sarah what was wrong. When they stopped at the master bedroom, James saw his father sitting on the side of the bed, staring out the window. James wanted to say something, but didn't know what to say. He closed the doors, then went back downstairs.

After an hour passed, James made sure Katy and Julie were all tucked into bed. Katy looked up at him, blue eyes wide open as if she could stay up all night. She clutched the picture of the dark figure next to her. "Do you see your friend, Katy?"

Katy nodded, looking over James' shoulder.

James turned, but saw nothing. "Can you talk to it?"

Katy nodded.

"What does it say, sweetheart?"

Katy took a loud breath, then turned on her side, whispered the words barely loud enough for James to hear, "He's got the whole, world, in his hands; He's got the whole wide world, in his hands . . ."

James looked behind him one more time, but only saw Julie in bed with her eyes closed. He turned back around, leaned over, gave Katy a kiss on the forehead, did the same to Julie, then went back downstairs, passing Samantha as she headed off to bed.

Jacob was watching Sportscenter when James plopped down on the couch next to him. Rebecca sat in the corner chair reading one of her books. James looked over to his brother. "Change to the news," he said.

"No. I don't want to watch any more of it—you saw it earlier—ask mom and dad about it tomorrow if you're so interested."

"Just turn it back, Jacob."

"It's probably not even on anymore."

"Then you have nothing to worry about, do you?"

"No, because I'm not gonna change it."

Rebecca rolled her eyes. "Don't start, you two."

James lunged for the remote, but Jacob swung it quickly under his arm.

"Will you two keep it down!" Rebecca said. "You'll wake up mom and dad."

James and Jacob started wrestling for control of the television. While doing so they accidentally turned it off. James finally pinned his brother's arm to the ground, then ripped the controller from his hand. Once he faced the t.v. to turn it back on, he saw reflected off the black screen a dark, shadowy figure standing in the kitchen. Turning suddenly, fear shot through his body like an electric current when the figure remained. He went to yell out, but could no longer control his voice.

Suddenly, James' whole body went stiff. His eyes looked over, saw Jacob and Rebecca trembling on the floor, frozen in place, just like him. Rebecca's toes curled towards the bottom on her feet, then his did the same, feeling as if they were bending in half. He wanted to yell out, but couldn't utter a sound.

Suddenly weightless, James' body straightened and slowly levitated until the tips of his toes were several feet from the family room floor. Then, Rebecca flew to his side, followed by Jacob. They hovered in place, turning slowly like they were hanging from a rotating rack.

James' body then violently locked into place: his hands outstretched, head tilted back, and his back arched like he was performing a swan dive. His clothes were then ripped from his body. He hovered naked, eyes to the sky, his heels and fingertips touching his brother's and sister's. He couldn't say or do anything.

Slowly, the pressure increased. The pain was excruciating, like each of his organs was swelling; like they were going to explode. His skin began to tear. At first the lacerations were small, but as the pressure built, the tears grew wider and their number increased, but did not bleed. Every second he felt more skin rip, but he couldn't cry out, or even cry.

His eyes suddenly rolled back into his head. As the pressure continued to build, the blood vessels popped and he could feel fluids dripping from his eyes and mouth. He then felt blood begin to pour from his torn skin.

Finally, his eyes were allowed to close. When they did, he saw the dark, shadowy figure staring back.

CHAPTER FOUR

Evil Escalating

Paul lay in bed, unable to sleep. He kept looking up to the ceiling, asking God what he'd done. Sarah tucked at his side, told him to try to sleep, but he couldn't. "Is this a test, Sarah . . . can this be a test?"

"It feels like one." She sat up and turned the light on. "I can't stop seeing that ugly mug. Part of me wishes you'd have hurt that man, Paul . . . I hate to say it, but it's true."

Paul saw Mark's face smiling, taunting. "I'll check tomorrow with the lawyers, see what they can do about getting our money back."

"I hope that man gets his someday."

Paul looked to his wife. "'Love your enemies and pray for those who persecute you, that you may be children of your Father in heaven.'"

Sarah scoffed. "I'm sorry Paul, but I'm in no mood for scripture."

Paul grabbed Sarah's hand resting over the covers. "Now's the best time for scripture, my love. Mathew, chapter five, 'God causes the sun to rise on the evil and the good, and sends rain on the righteous and the unrighteous.' Never forget, sweetheart, God works in mysterious ways."

"So too does Satan," she grumbled.

"Indeed, my love, which is why we must remain steadfast in our faith and not let this evil deception work on us. I love you, Sarah, and I promise we'll figure this out. We'll get through this and be the stronger for it, we always have."

"Mom," whispered Julie, peaking her little head through the open door. "Mom."

"What is it?"

"Katy won't stop singing."

Sarah took a deep breath and pushed off the bed to get up, but Paul gently grabbed her wrist. "Stay in bed, sweetheart. I'll get up. I can't sleep anyway."

"Are you sure?"

"Yup . . . see . . . I'm already out of bed."

Paul followed Julie back to her room, but when they arrived, Katy appeared to be fast asleep. "Katy," Paul called out softly. "Katy, are you faking?" Katy snored a little louder. "Get back in bed," Paul said to Julie.

Julie did. Paul then approached Katy and knelt by the side of her bed. "I believe you can hear me, Katy, so stop the singing for tonight," he said in a whisper. "If I have to come back in here, you will be in trouble. Do I make myself clear?"

He waited a few moments.

"Yes, daddy," Katy said in a whisper. "I'm sorry."

"Okay. Now, go to sleep." Paul walked over to Julie. "You too, little one."

"I can't sleep now," Julie said.

"Well, you can get up and get some water. That should help, okay?"

"Okay," Julie said, but stayed in bed.

Paul smiled, then left their room. There were lights on downstairs in the kitchen, but he didn't hear the television. He took one step in that direction before turning around and heading back to his room. His eldest children could wait till tomorrow to know what happened. He kissed Sarah on the forehead, then tucked himself into bed.

"Are they alright," Sarah asked, sounding like she was nearly asleep.

"They're fine," Paul said, then closed his eyes and tried to get some sleep.

He just got comfortable when a blood curdling scream sounded. "Get up Paul!" Sarah said frantically as the scream carried on.

Paul sprung from the bed, rushed to the stairs, saw Julie standing at the bottom of the staircase screaming at the top of her lungs and looking through the arch that separated the foyer from the kitchen. "Julie!" Paul yelled running down the stairs. He grabbed her, shook her out of her scream. "What is it darling?" Following her eyes into the family room, Paul thought for a moment he was having a nightmare. Never before had he felt so instantly frozen. James, Rebecca and Jacob were bloodied and hovering above the ground, slowly turning and dripping blood from their toes, their naked bodies covered with hideous lacerations. Below them was a massive pool of blood that almost extended the entire wooden floor.

"What is it darling?" Sarah asked upon reaching the bottom of the stairs.

Paul felt her dig her nails into his shoulder, but he couldn't move. He shook uncontrollably, didn't even look over when Sarah fell to the ground. Finally, he yelled out, screaming for his children as loud as he could. "NO!" he cried out running into the family room, his bare feet nearly slipping on the blood. Just as he reached out and touched Jacob's ankle, all three lifeless bodies fell to the ground.

***

It took a little under ten minutes for the firetruck to arrive, another few for the ambulance. Even the veterans had to take a minute when they first saw the bodies—the youngest EMT needed to throw up before he could help. Two more ambulances were called when, to the shock of everyone, James, Rebecca and Jacob still had the slightest of pulses.

The police showed up not long after the first ambulance.

"Like I said," Paul kept repeating, "when my wife and I went downstairs, we saw them *hovering in the air*!"

The detective nodded slowly while he wrote the statement down. "You were the first to see them?"

"No. Our daughter, Julie, screamed when she went into the kitchen," Paul said, then looked over to his little girl. Julie stood next to his wife, her eyes staring straight forward, but it was as if she didn't see anything in front of her.

"Can I speak with her?" the detective asked.

Paul shook his head. "She hasn't spoken to anyone . . . not even her mother."

"All the same," persisted the detective, "I'd like to try."

Behind Julie and Sarah were the other children, faces filled with tears. The detective walked up, got down on his knee, touched Julie softly on the hand. "Hello there sweetheart, my name is detective Roberts. Can you tell me yours?" Julie didn't answer. She didn't even look at him. "I know you've been through a lot tonight, and that I must seem like a burden to you, but you would be helping everyone if you could answer my questions."

Julie looked at the detective.

The detective smiled, asked, "What did you see?"

Julie screamed. Sarah cradled the child and told the detective to leave her alone.

The detective stood up from his knelt position and pulled Paul aside. "We have counseling available, not only for Julie, but for all of you . . . if you want it."

Paul nodded. "Thank you, detective."

Detective Roberts raised an eyebrow. "Okay, now, here comes the standard questions. Have you made any recent enemies?" Paul shook his head, but the detective looked back sternly, eyes full of disbelief. "Is there anyone, recent or long standing, who might have wished you or your family ill?"

Paul shook his head. "Nothing like this."

"Have you noticed anything strange over the past few days—anything out of the usual?" Paul rubbed his face as the day replayed in his head. "Anything at all," urged the detective.

The more he replayed the day's events in his head, the more they seemed part of a nightmare that couldn't be real. Finally, he nodded slowly. "I think my wife and I were robbed—"

"Robbed," detective Roberts interrupted. "Well, that's definitely worth looking into. Can you tell me about it?"

Paul wished for a moment he'd have simply lied. "I don't know what to say. Someone who looked like me walked into the bank and withdrew my money . . . all of it . . ."

The detective nodded. "I heard about that. Is there anything else?"

Paul remembered the dark figure. "I saw . . . something."

"Something? Can you be more specific, Mr. Bellomy?"

"It was dark, like a shadow . . . but not the shadow of a person . . .. It was . . . I don't know how to describe it . . . it was a dark, shadowy form . . . life-like—"

The detective raised his hand. "Okay, Mr. Bellomy, that's enough for now. I've written down the information; we'll start with what we have. Here's my card. Give me a call if you remember anything else. We'll be in touch."

Paul saw the look in the detective's face, his dark eyes laughing at the unbelievable testimony. "I'm not lying, detective."

Roberts chuckled. "I never said you were."

As the detective walked away, Paul saw the faces of the officers standing around. Each one looked at him, accusing him with their eyes, and Paul had just told the detective that he robbed himself and was seeing strange, unbelievable images. He started wondering if he was indeed going crazy.

Paul walked over to his family as the paramedics rolled James out into the first ambulance. "James!" Sarah cried out, just as Paul wrapped his arms around her. "James!"

"Julie, I'm sorry," Katy said. Paul looked down, saw Katy pulling on Julie's shirt. "Julie, I'm sorry for singing earlier . . . please forgive me."

"Forgive Katy, Julie," Adam said, red-eyed from crying so much. "You have to."

"Guys, knock it off," Paul snapped as the medics wheeled Rebecca out. "Damn it—kids, come over here." Paul huddled them in the garage, keeping their red faces away from seeing Jacob being wheeled out and secured in the last ambulance.

"Julie, please," Katy begged.

"Katy, Julie forgives you, okay sweetheart," Sarah said.

"But, *she needs* to say it."

Sarah kissed Julie on the forehead. "You forgive your sister, don't you baby?"

Julie kept quiet, the only eyes not reddened by tears.

"Samantha," Paul said strongly, hoping to show strength to his children. "Your mother and I need to go to the hospital now. The police are going to stay here while we're away. I need you to make sure your brothers and sisters get to bed, okay?"

Samantha shook her head, still crying.

Paul went to a knee, took Samantha and Bryan in his arms, then looked over each one of his children. "Be strong," Paul said, holding back his own tears. "Either James . . ." the names were hard to say out loud, "Rebecca . . . and Jacob will live and everything will be alright . . .. Or, they will pass on to God's loving arms. Hey," he made sure each of his children looked him in the eyes, even Julie. "Hey, as we learned from John, chapter four, verse eighteen: 'There is no fear in love; but perfect love casteth out fear: because fear hath torment. He that feareth is not made perfect in love.'" Paul kissed the forehead of each of his children. "Love your brothers and sister, do not fear for them, okay? Can you do that for me, and for them?"

Five heads slowly nodded, even Julie's.

Paul closed his eyes for only a moment to pray silently. *Lord, whatever wisdom is in your divine plan, please let it show itself soon. For my family's sake, please Lord.*

The paramedics were just about to take off.

Paul opened his eyes, mustered all his fortitude, and took Sarah by the hand. "We should go," he said with a nod.

Before Paul and Sarah got in their car to follow the ambulance, Katy ran up to her mother and father. "Mommy, mommy," cried Katy. "Take me with you; take us all with you."

Sarah cried.

"No baby," Paul answered, returning to a knee. "You stay here and listen to your sister. Samantha is in charge until we get home." Paul walked Katy back to the garage and put her hand in Samantha's. He then walked up to the sergeant and asked if he would leave an extra unit at the house until they returned. The officer agreed.

The sirens flashed as the ambulance took off down the Bellomy's driveway. Paul and Sarah followed closely, Paul watching the children huddled around the house window from the rearview mirror. Three police cars sat in the driveway, six total officers roamed the property. Once they made the left hand turn on the main road, Sarah again broke down in tears.

Speeding down the road, passing the bright yellow street lights, following the flashing red lights of the ambulances—Paul fell into a trance. Everything seemed fake. Everything moved too fast to be real, but also moved too slow.

A dark, shadowy figure stood under one of the streetlights.

Paul slammed the brakes.

"What are you doing?" screamed Sarah as Paul stopped dead in the street.

Paul turned, looked through the back window. "Did you see that?"

"See what?"

Paul got out of the car and looked again.

"What are you doing?"

"It was right there!" Paul yelled.

"What was there?"

"It was right there," Paul whispered, pointing to the exact spot where he'd seen the shadow. "It was right there."

"Get in the car!"

Frustrated, fearing he was loosing his mind, Paul got back in the car and continued on to the hospital.

Fifteen minutes after getting to the hospital, while sitting anxiously in the waiting room, legs rapidly bouncing, Paul came to a conclusion. "I think I was possessed," he said.

Sarah turned to him, her face flushed and pale. "What?"

"I can't think of anything else. Nothing else makes sense. I can't remember anything until about three o' clock in the afternoon. I've seen a dark, shadowy figure twice today—once before I met you at the bank; the other while we drove here. I don't know what it is. I think it's something evil. I think it's targeted me . . . or the family."

"You're scaring me," Sarah said, her lower lip trembling.

Paul looked to his trembling hands. "I'm scaring myself."

"What do we do?"

Paul hesitated, but there was only one thing that he could think to do. "We must pray."

Sarah shook her head, a hint of contempt glaring from her green eyes. "I've been praying nonstop since this afternoon," she said bitterly.

Paul snapped a sharp eye her way. "We mustn't lose faith."

Sarah shook her head, then looked away.

Five minutes later a doctor approached. "I'm sorry," she said. "There was . . . nothing we could do."

Sarah fell to the ground and cried aloud. Paul caught her on her way down and held her in his arms. "WHY?" Sarah screamed, her eyes looking upward.

Paul cried with his wife, who kept yelling the question.

"We have counseling available if you feel the need," offered the doctor. Her nurse interrupted and told her that she was needed with another patient. She again apologized for the Bellomy's loss before leaving.

Paul and Sarah sat on the floor, holding each other and crying for a good ten minutes. Random people walked by. Some stared before walking away.

Paul's cell phone went off. When he looked at the number, he did not recognize it, and did not answer. When the same number called again, almost right after he rejected the first call, he answered. "Hello," he could barely say.

"Mr. Bellomy?"

"Yes."

"This is officer Smith."

"Yes, officer."

"Sir . . . I don't know how to tell you this . . ."

"Tell me what, officer?" Paul could hear the officer breathing heavily on the other end of the phone. "Tell me what?" Paul said sharply.

Sarah looked up, her pale face turned even whiter.

"Sir . . ."

"What?" Paul yelled.

"There was a . . . a fire . . . and . . ."

Paul went cold.

"I'm so sorry, Mr. Bellomy . . . but, there was nothing we could do—it spread too fast . . .. We couldn't get them in time . . ."

The phone fell from his hand. Lunging forward, kneeling, Paul struggled for air. His chest burned and felt like someone was squeezing his heart in their hand. The immense pressure was unbearable.

"What is it?" Sarah asked. "What's wrong?"

Paul couldn't talk.   His whole body went numb. Sarah picked up the phone. "Hello? Hello? . . . What are you talking about? What spread too fast?"

The room started spinning. Paul saw Sarah throw the phone against the wall, braking it into several pieces before screaming at the top of her lungs.   Then, everything went dark.

CHAPTER FIVE

Evil Taunting

Paul's chest pain turned out to be an angina. The doctors gave him a prescription and recommended that he not drive home if he didn't have to. Since Sarah was in no condition to drive either, a police car was sent to the hospital to pick them up.

The ride home did not feel like a ride home. The word home no longer meant the same thing. When the police car passed the light where Paul earlier saw the shadow, he saw nothing. He feared he was loosing his mind. He feared Sarah already had. When he noticed that she was staring straight into the back of the driver's seat, eyes glazed, he saw a broken woman.

Paul surveyed the damage as the police car drove up the driveway. The morning fog made the already eerie scene even more frightful. The guest cottage was untouched, but only the foundational beams of the main home stood, blackened by fire, as if the house was an ancient ruin.

"Mr. Bellomy," said a man, hand outstretched as Paul got out from the back of the police car. "I'm the fire investigator."

Paul nodded. "How did this happen."

The investigator shook his head. "We don't know yet . . . none of it is making sense. There doesn't seem to be a cause, as strange as that sounds. Every piece of data I have suggests the whole thing just suddenly went up in flames. Everything at the same time."

"What do you mean?"

"I don't know," whispered the investigator. "According to the police officers who saw it, the whole things was normal one-second, then completely aflame the next. The fire captain said the flames just, well, stopped before they should have, like someone put a giant lid over the house. Everything I've seen is consistent with that testimony, but I can't begin to explain it. What's even stranger is the temperature the fire had to burn at . . . there's no way everything should've burnt as thoroughly as it did in that time . . . this wasn't a normal fire . . ."

As the detective continued, Paul could only think of his children, screaming, stuck in the inferno, frightened beyond belief.

" . . . I'll let you know if I find anything else," the investigator said, then walked away.

Paul stood next to Sarah in their driveway, eyes fixed upon what used to be their house. Every piece of foundation exhibited the same degree of damage.

Everything that wasn't foundational no longer existed. All that was left on the ground was a pile of ashes. A slight wind carried charred pieces and scattered them amongst the fog.

Paul would've cried, but he and Sarah had long since cried themselves out of tears. All that remained were blank stares—blank minds that, when active, only had questions. They did not hold each other. Anytime Paul reached for Sarah's hand, she pulled away.

Hours passed with Paul just sitting next to Sarah on the guest cottage couch. Since the police officer called the previous night, neither had spoken a word to the other.

Paul stared out the window, looking at the visible remains of what he used to call home. It was the children, not the house, that was on his mind. He could only stare at the blackened four-by-fours and four-by-twos that once made a wall and an apex of a roof. That area used to be the family room, where the children would congregate after school and dinner. Although the foundation still stood, it no longer served a purpose other than to torment.

Another hour passed. The first of many calls arrived a little past eight-thirty in the morning. Paul didn't even look to see who it was.

Paul sat at the kitchen table in the cottage and stared blankly at the wall. He was stuck in a pattern of sitting or standing in a place for about ten minutes before moving on to a different location. The pattern slowly brought him closer to his old house. He had started in the upstairs bedroom and now got up from the table and walked outside. He sat on the step and stared at what was left of the old house's frame. He used to love these foggy mornings, especially as the sun began slowly shining through. This morning, however, the fog persisted, too thick for the feeble rays of light to penetrate.

Paul rose from the step and slowly walked. He did not consciously mean to head towards the ruins, but that was where he ended up. As Paul traveled the short distance of about fifty yards, the entire structure of the old house became visible.

Paul stepped over a short mound of brick as he entered what used to be the family room. The fire place was still standing and the metal from the furniture gave markers to the now open area. As Paul walked he stirred up the ashes from the ground. Finally, he could go no further, and he fell to his knees. His heart began pounding. He needed to calm himself down.

After taking a few slow, deep breaths, Paul continued to kneel in the ashes. After a few moments, he dug both hands into the ground. He did not know where his children lay, but he threw a fistful of ashes upon himself. "Almighty Father, eternal God, hear my prayer for Your children whom You have called from this life to Yourself. Grant them light, happiness, and peace. Let them pass in safety through the gates of death, and live forever with all Your saints in the light You promised to Abraham and to all his descendants in faith. Guard them from all harm and on that great day of resurrection and reward raise them up with all Your saints. Pardon their sins and give them eternal life in Your kingdom. I ask this through Christ our Lord. Amen."

Paul bent down and kissed the ground, thinking of his children, thinking of the shadow that took them from him. Paul raised his head and drew a cross in the ground. He felt the sorrow, but he had no more tears that would fall on the ashes.

Just then, he heard subtle sounds all around him, but he didn't see anything. The sound was heard again. "Come for me you son of a bitch; come for me you evil spirit!"

The sounds got closer, like soft creeping steps. Paul yearned for the shadow to show itself, hoping to either smite the enemy with a righteous hand, or die in the process. "Show yourself!" Paul yelled, just as a shadow appeared in the distance. It was approaching from the driveway. Paul trembled and breathed heavily as the sounds grew louder, readying himself for the worst.

Just then, Paul's chest pounded and felt like someone again was squeezing it. Keeling over from the pain, things became fuzzy. "Paul," sounded a voice. Paul grabbed his chest and tried to calm himself, but his surrounding began to spin. "Paul," again sounded the voice.

The shadow emerged from the fog. Paul squinted his eyes to try to make out what was before him. The figure's pace quickened. In a matter of moments it was upon Paul. "Paul!" yelled Stan. "Is that you?"

Paul's agent emerged from the fog, knelt beside him in the ashes. "My god!" exclaimed Stan. "Are you alright?" Paul could only shake his head. Stan brushed off some of the ashes and dirt from Paul's body.

"Stan . . . what are you doing here?"

"I'm truly sorry. I'd been trying to get ahold of you since yesterday morning. When I heard what happened, I figured I'd just stop by. I didn't mean to scare you, but you had the gate locked, so I thought I'd just walk in to check up on you."

"My phone broke."

"That's fine, I'm just concerned . . . how are you?"

Paul looked up, astonished at the question. "I'm terrible.... I lost everything.... My children are gone . . .."

"Look, Paul, I didn't come here to put you through more grief. I just wanted to check up on you and let you know that I and everyone at the office is here for you if you need us."

Paul nodded, whispered, "Thank you."

"Don't worry about the book. We can put that off until you're ready."

"I don't care about the book—the book can burn for all I care . . ."

"I understand," Stan said, patting Paul's shoulder. "I just wanted to let you know." The two men sat quietly in the middle of the old family room, fog, ash and debris surrounding them. Stan nodded, "Well, if you'd rather be alone." He got to his feet and placed his hand on Paul's shoulder. "If you need anything, we're here for you."

Even in his moment of grief, Paul still did not wish to seem rude to someone who came to offer their condolences and support. He rose to his feet and thanked his agent.

"I'm truly sorry for your loss," grieved Stan one final time.

"Thank you," accepted Paul.

Stan turned and headed back down the driveway, Paul watching as he slowly became a distant shadow before completely disappearing.

Paul turned slowly, jumped back when he faced a small-darkened form no more than two feet from him. Paul turned his head and cringed from the sight. When he looked back, the form extended its hand. Paul recoiled, fell to the ashes cowering. When Paul looked closer he saw that the figure appeared to be a little girl. She was burned from head to toe. Her charred body stood in pain, mouth opened, but no words followed. Paul looked closer, finally recognizing his little girl, Samantha. Suddenly, it spoke.

"Daddy!"

"NO!" Paul yelled, turning away. When he looked again, she was gone.

His chest again pounded and his head fell back to the ground. He looked up to the heavens and cried out, not with tears, but with a yearning for his little girl—for all of his children. Images of the three lacerated bodies, their bloodshot eyes and torn skin, tormented his thoughts. Now he had the image of his younger children, burnt completely. The pain from his chest seemed to be holding him down. If he had the choice, he would save himself the pain and end it at that very moment. As he stared up to the sky, he prayed to God that he was having a heart attack.

***

Sarah finally turned off her ringing phone. She knew she would not be able to avoid people forever. However, she could not get herself to talk with those who would only have questions—questions to which she did not have answers. She felt an uncontrollable urge to lash out at something; anything. She felt like a completely different person.

She got up from the couch and stood by the window. She could barely see Paul lying amongst the ruins—his outstretched arm reached towards the sky. "'Indeed, God does not listen to their empty pleas; the Almighty pays no attention to it. They cried for help, but there was no one to save them—to the LORD, but He did not answer.'"

Sarah closed her eyes, thought of her children. She saw them running and playing in the yard, Paul throwing a football to his sons.

Her eyes opened.

Like someone snapped their fingers and set her free, Sarah realized what was going on. "Paul," she whispered. She ran to the counter to get the prescribed drugs. "God dammit!" she yelled while fumbling around her purse. Finally, she found the prescription. She darted for the door, but when she turned the handle, she heard a voice calling to her.

"Mommy," it whispered.

Sarah turned. There was nothing there. She looked over everything in sight, slowly pulled the door open.

"Mommy," whispered the voice again.

Her hands shook, lower lip quivered as she took deep and heavy breaths. She could hear children laughing.

"Mommy," whispered the voice, each time getting a little louder, this time with the laughter of a child.

Sarah heard footsteps in the small two-story house. She heard the voices of her little ones laughing. She stared down the narrow hallway of the guest house into the large room at its end. She heard footsteps coming from the upstairs bedroom. When she looked to the ceiling, a figure darted across the doorway of the far room.

"Julie," yelled Sarah. "Is that you?"

Laughter came from the far room. Sarah took her hand off the doorknob and slowly walked down the hall.

"Mommy, we're here, with you," a voice said laughing.

"Julie, sweetheart, is that you?" asked Sarah as her pace quickened to the far room. Laughter was heard as Sarah entered the room, but no one was there. "Julie, where are you?" Laughter persisted as the sound of footsteps climbed up the narrow staircase. Sarah turned to look but could see no one. "Julie, baby, don't hide from me!" She went to the stairway and charged up to the single upstairs room. "Baby, it's gonna be alright! Mommy's coming for you!"

When she got upstairs she saw nothing but the bed and a few dressers. Laughter came from downstairs. Sarah screamed. "Don't hide from me!"

"But, mommy, we just want to play."

Footsteps could be heard downstairs, racing all around the lower story. Sarah again screamed, wanting to give up and remain curled in the corner; but, her motherly instincts kicked in—she could not give up on her children. She again breathed deep and charged downstairs. "Julie!" she yelled, now in a frenzy. She turned around as the footsteps and laughter seemed to surround her, but she saw nothing. She fell to the floor in desperation, looked to the ceiling as if it were the heavens. "Help me! Please, help me!"

Just then, a figure darted by the window outside the guest house. Sarah saw it clearly this time—it was her little Julie. "Baby! Stop running—I'm coming for you!"

Sarah got to her feet and stormed out the door. She heard the laughter and footsteps around the corner. She took off as fast as she could to try to catch up with it. When she turned the corner, she fell back in fear.

"Sarah!" Paul cried out, taking her in his arms. "Sarah, what is it? I heard you screaming—what happened?"

"No!" Sarah cried. "Let me go—I need to find her!"

Paul held tight, not letting her loose. "Find who, Sarah?"

"I saw her! I saw her! She was there, you must let me go!"

"Who? Sarah, who? Who did you see?"

Sarah buried her face in Paul's chest and screamed, pounding her fists on his shoulders as they both fell to their knees. Paul ran his hands through her hair and told her that everything would be alright. Sarah, surprisingly, began calming down. It was like a switch went off in her head. "We can get through this," Paul whispered in her ear.

After a few moments, Sarah's breaths slowed and she turned her head outwards while resting it on Paul's shoulder. "Get through this?" Sarah asked dryly. "How can we get through this?"

Paul held her close and tight. He dug his fingertips into her back as he rubbed it, every now and then grabbing a small handful of flesh. "Don't quit now, sweetheart; don't give up faith at the moment when it is so desperately needed."

Sarah scoffed. "Faith? In what should I have *faith*?"

"In God."

Sarah's grip around her husband weakened as Paul spoke. She still had her arms wrapped around his back, but she had no desire to hold on. "There is no God," Sarah said, laughing under her breath as she stared out upon her burnt-down home, her head resting comfortably upon Paul's shoulder.

CHAPTER SIX

Evil Tempting

Paul feared for Sarah, prayed God would cure her faltering faith with a sign that not all hope was lost. They both spent most of their time in the guest cottage, both making trips every couple hours back to the ruins. At times they would go together, sometimes not. Conversation was minimal.

They endured surprise visits from friends and family. Paul appreciated the sentiments of loved ones, but Sarah was noticeably cold to every guest. She began responding to messages on her phone simply to keep people from showing up unannounced.

Insurance, police and fire detectives crowded the grounds most of the next day. A whole slew of reporters and other various investigators foamed at the mouth outside the front gate. When a brazen journalist worked up the courage to trespass, he was arrested. Few other attempts were made; neither Paul nor Sarah made a statement.

Paul and Sarah talked to people only when there was no other option. The insurance investigator received minimal cooperation. The police received the same. The only people who Paul took any interest in were the fire investigators. Still, they were at a loss for a cause. The insurance investigators were counting heavily on the findings of the fire crew. With speculation running wild about Paul and Sarah's mental states, the cause of the fire would be a crucial factor in the insurance company's decision whether to and how much to compensate for damages.

Hours passed.

Paul stood by the window, watching as the moon cast an eerie light over the ruins. He looked back at Sarah sleeping on the couch, wishing he too could fall asleep. He hadn't slept in well over a day. Every time he closed his eyes he saw Samantha; not the beautiful young lady, but the burnt image of a suffering child. If it wasn't Samantha, he saw another one of his children, each one in the same condition, or worse.

"Dad," a voice whispered.

Paul closed his eyes again, prayed for his children's salvation. Every time a voice whispered to him, he issued a prayer for his children.

Feeling the increasing pull of the ruins upon him, Paul's eyes opened. Ever since the authorities left for the day, he felt the pull, increasing more as the minutes ticked by.

"Dad," a voice whispered.

Paul closed his eyes when he heard Adam's voice and prayed once more. His eyes opened quickly when the image of his son's charred body pierced his mind.

Looking back out the window, Paul stepped back and dropped his glass of water. The shadow stood amongst the ruins. There were no eyes, but it was as if it looked at Paul, as if it pulled on him, calling Paul to it.

"Sarah," Paul mumbled, then quickly shot a glance her way. She was still sleeping on the couch. When he looked back out the window, the shadow had disappeared.

Paul stared out the window for several minutes, searching for the shadow, resisting the pull tugging him back to the ruins. "Fine," he finally mumbled. He kissed Sarah on the forehead, then walked the paved path leading to the ruins, his eyes scanning the darkness for the shadow. "Show yourself," Paul whispered.

Approaching the border of what used to be his family room, he rested his hand on the blackened foundational beam. It was still sturdy. "I'm here," Paul said, stepping into the borders of his old family room. "Where are you?"

Paul heard a snap behind him, turned, backed further into the old room, then stopped himself. He closed his eyes and took a deep breath. When his eyes opened again, he was certain he was in a dream.

Paul stood in the corner of his family room, light blue walls standing like they were freshly painted. The walls and ceiling were up. The house looked just as it did before he and Sarah decided to move in fifteen years ago. It was empty, but whole.

Paul touched the wall, quickly pulled his hand back when the wall felt real. "What is this?" he mumbled.

Turning again, he faced his kitchen, then hesitantly began walking through his home. Laughter could be heard all around him. When he turned to look, no one could be seen. Walking through the kitchen, he stared out into the backyard, saw sun shining on the grass and the barbecue out and ready to be used.

When Paul looked back, furniture and appliances decorated the previously empty spaces. It looked just as it had before. The couch was exactly the same and positioned right in the middle of the family room, the pots and pans hung over the kitchen's center island, the television hung right over the fireplace. The television turned on. A football game was just starting the third quarter.

Laughter and footsteps came from upstairs. Paul slowly walked towards the arch that separated the kitchen from the entryway. As he walked he let his hand rub the railing that separated the kitchen from the family room. The footsteps charged down the stairs.

"You kids need to go outside and play," Sarah said with a laugh.

Paul froze. Sarah looked like an angel, as she seemed to glide into the kitchen. She walked right up to Paul and gave him a kiss. Their eyes met, Paul wishing somehow everything around him was real. *Is this heaven? Did I die?*

Sarah smiled, made her way to the refrigerator and took out the makings for a sandwich. "Would you like one?" she asked.

"What is this?"

"It's just turkey and ham," Sarah said with a laugh. "You don't have to eat if you don't want to."

"No . . .. This . . ." Paul gestured with his hands, pointing out everything around him. "What is this?"

Sarah dipped the knife in mayonnaise and moistened the bread. "This is our home."

"Our home?" Paul scoffed. "Who are you?"

Sarah raised an eyebrow, took the mustard and squirted some on the bread. She laughed playfully when Paul just stared at her.

"Who are you?"

"I'm your wife, Paul."

Paul nodded in disbelief. "Of course you are." He took a step towards the kitchen's center island where Sarah was making the sandwiches and rested his right hand on the countertop. "And, I suppose, those are our children I hear upstairs?"

"Of course they are," she said pilling the meat and cheese on the bread. "Why would you ask such a thing?" She cut the sandwich in half and took a bite. "When are you planning on starting the barbecue?"

"Why make a sandwich if I'm supposed to barbecue?"

"I don't feel like having a hot dog or hamburger," replied Sarah. "What's wrong with you? You seem . . . different." Four children ran down the stairs. They were laughing and playing and seemed to be having a great time. "I told you little blessings to take it outside," Sarah said with a laugh, rubbing each of their heads as they ran past, out to the back yard. One stopped and tried to take a piece of meat before heading into the back yard. Sarah lightly smacked his hand. "No, no, young man," she playfully reprimanded the little boy. "You're going to have daddy's barbecue; you don't need this."

The little boy smiled and carried on.

"Dad," said the boy, "do you want to play with us before you begin cooking?"

Paul wanted to smile at the little lad, but couldn't. He just stared at the four young children, all looking in some ways like him and Sarah, but all completely different from what he was expecting; all completely different from the children he once had.

"Daddy will be out in a little while," Sarah answered for Paul.

"Okay," said the little boy before running off into the backyard.

"Daddy," asked the little girl, running up to the screen door, "when you begin cooking, can I have an extra piece of cheese on my hamburger?"

Again, Paul could not respond.

"I think we can make that happen," answered Sarah, who took another bite of her sandwich after the little girl joined her siblings on the back grass. "They really would love to play with you."

"Stop! Whatever this is, I want it to stop."

"What are you talking about? We're your family, Paul . . . this can't stop."

"This is *not* my family," Paul snapped. "Those are not my children. I've never seen them in my life."

Sarah put her sandwich down, approached Paul. "Now, my love, you need to take a few deep breaths. The doctor said when you feel like this you need to take your pills—have you taken them today?"

Paul shook his head, backing away.

"Paul, it's been almost ten years since that happened. We got through it—we had more children—we carried on." She approached Paul and rubbed his hair and scruffy face with her hand. "This is your family," she persisted, staring deep into his blue eyes. "You were right. We kept the faith, and look at what's happened."

Paul looked deep into Sarah's green eyes, the same eyes he had loved for decades; but something was different. A darkness emerged from behind them, a darkness he could sense only intuitively. Part of him still wished this was real; part of him would not be able to stand it if it were. "No," he whispered. Sarah backed away. "This is *not* real!" Paul shook his head. "This isn't real."

Sarah shrugged. "It could be. All this could be real."

Paul shook his head. "Who are you? What are you?"

"Does that matter? You can have a family again; you can have everything that was ever lost—isn't that all that matters?"

Paul shook his head. A tear fell when he thought of everything that was lost. "I don't want *another* family." His breath quickened, his heart began to pound. Clenching his fist, he dug his fingernails into his palm and glared at the figure before him pretending to be his wife. He shook his head, his teeth grinding with hatred.

"Paul, *you* need a family."

"I HAD A FAMILY!"

His racing heart knocked him to a knee. When he looked up, Sarah was gone; the house was empty. The walls still stood, but nothing was inside. It was again an empty house.

As Paul's breaths slowly deepened his chest pain decreased. He gripped the railing to help him back to his feet. There was no more sound—no laughter or footsteps. When he looked out the kitchen door he saw only darkness.

Paul slowly started walking through the kitchen, pausing briefly when he approached the archway leading to the foyer, and looked out the front window as he neared the staircase. Again, only darkness existed through the glass.

Eyes were on him, he could feel it. A single framed family photo sat on top of the glass table in the sitting room. The stairs to his back, Paul went to the photo. He looked at his entire family—his sons, his daughters, his wife. He picked up the photo and held it in both hands.

Paul turned with his head buried in the image of his family, his finger tip running over each one individually, touching the face of his sons and daughters. A tear fell upon the photo, right in the center of his family.

"Daddy."

Paul looked up, dropped the framed photo. The glass cracked upon hitting the ground, a line sent straight through his family. Standing at the top of the staircase was little Katy. Julie, Adam, Bryan and Samantha were also spread out along the second floor railing. Paul closed his eyes, but he could still see them.

"Daddy," whispered Katy.

"Daddy," whispered Adam.

Paul opened his eyes but looked at the floor. He wanted to run up the stairs and hug them, even if they weren't real. But he couldn't move.

"Daddy," whispered Julie.

"Daddy," whispered Bryan.

Paul put his hands to his head, pulled on his hair. "You're not real . . .. This is all in my head; this is all a trick."

"No trick, father," Samantha said. "It is us."

Paul looked up, broke down and cried gazing again upon their faces, and was unable to stay away. "Children," Paul whispered approaching the staircase. "I'm so sorry."

"Why daddy?" asked Katy. "Did you do this?"

"No . . . I would never hurt any of you—I love you all, more than—"

"Stop!" Samantha snapped as Paul was about to place his foot on the bottom step. "You can't come up here."

"Why?"

"We can't be with you anymore," Adam said sharply.

"I just want to say goodbye . . . please—"

"Goodbye, daddy," said Julie.

"No, sweetheart, not like that—I want more than that." He put his hand on the stair railing and his foot on the bottom step.

"NO!" Samantha yelled.

The stairs slowly turned to ash. They began crumbling as the ash crawled up towards his children.

"You were told you can't come up here," Katy scolded.

The crawling ash came to the top of the stairs, right where Katy stood. The ash overcame her, covering her body, turning her into a charred remnant of what she'd been. Slowly the ash overcame all Paul's children. The entire house turned to ash as the eyeless glare of his five children terrified his soul.

"Daddy," whispered all the children. "Daddy . . . daddy . . ."

All of a sudden, as from a whirlwind, the children blew apart, just like the house around them. "NO!" Paul yelled, then charged forward until he was thrown back, hitting hard against something, then everything went black.

Paul's eyes slowly opened to Sarah rocking back and forth beside him. "Perhaps you're the lucky one," he heard her say.

"Sarah," Paul mumbled, his vision clearing. It was dark, he and Sarah were covered in ashes. He glanced over his shoulder, saw the remnants of the brick fireplace behind him.

"Paul . . . are you sure you want to wake up?"

Paul shivered, was still a little dazed. "What are you talking about?" he asked sitting himself upright. He rubbed the back of his head to make sure he wasn't bleeding. "What happened?"

Sarah laughed, then pursed her lips to a frown. "That's only one of the questions I don't have an answer to."

Paul looked over, to Sarah rocking back and forth. "Sarah, are you alright?"

Sarah chuckled. "Asks the man I just found lying unconscious amongst his family's ruins."

Paul took a deep breath, got to his feet.

"Daddy," whispered a voice.

Paul looked frantically. "Did you hear that? Sarah, did you hear that?"

"I hear the emptiness," she lamented. "I hear the cries of those who were abandoned, just like we've been . . . and will continue to be."

Paul felt his stomach tie in knots. On top of everything else, he was losing his wife. "Come on,

Sarah," Paul said, gripping Sarah under her armpits to hoist her up. "Come on, let's go back inside."

Hours passed before Paul tried to sleep. Sarah had gone to bed once they returned to the guest cottage, but when Paul finally crawled into bed, he could only lay awake staring at the ceiling. He looked over at Sarah again. Ashes still colored her face, but she slept out the night as if she'd never had children.

Was Sarah the shadow? Was he talking with the devil? Was the shadow a demon, sent by the devil? Was he imagining the whole thing? Was he still imagining?

"Daddy," whispered the voice.

The voices would not stop calling him. Not only did they torment him, they pulled on him to return. Even when they did not whisper to him, he felt himself drawn to the grounds of his old home.

Paul got out of bed and put on blue jeans and a plain white t-shirt, then went downstairs to the window and looked again to the ruins. The shadow was there, standing on top of Paul's sacred ground. He could feel it calling him back, taunting him to return.

Paul's fear was gone, replaced by a hatred, a deep, grinding desire for retribution. There was no hesitation: he stormed out the door. As he approached the ruins, the figure vanished, but the pull was as strong as ever. Paul continued on without hesitation, stepped into the ashes as if they were the hollowed grounds of his ultimate battleground.

Once he stepped over the border, he was back in the empty but standing house. It was just as it had been before he made the mistake of trying to go upstairs. "Where are you?" Paul slowly walked through the family room, continued through the kitchen, under the archway and to the stairs. "Are you here?"

There was no answer.

Paul wouldn't try going upstairs again. Instead, he walked down the hallway towards the garage. When he approached the door, the handle was stiff and resisted being opened. When he gripped the handle tighter, the door flung open on its own.

The garage was empty, just like the rest of the house. He took a few moments to inspect every corner before closing the door.

Paul turned around, then jumped back against the door. A horribly grotesque figure stood before him. Paul looked away, knowing what he'd just seen. It was his son, James, all bloodied and lacerated with his eyes rolled back in his head. When Paul finally stomached another look, James had disappeared.

"Leave my family alone . . . let them rest in peace!"

Paul slowly walked back down the hall towards the kitchen. Upon approaching the archway that divided the foyer and the kitchen, his right arm trembled and his courage began fading. He stared upon his three oldest children. They were hovering above the family room ground, shoulder to shoulder, spinning slowly, heads facing the ceiling, heels touching. Their arms were to their sides, chests extended, but their mangled bodies were dry, like treated corpses.

"Stop this . . . please . . . I beg you . . ."

Paul moved again, felt like he too hovered as he approached his children. His feet stepped on the blood-filled floor, his shaky voice calling their names as each of his children faced him.

"James . . . Rebecca . . . Jacob . . ."

As Rebecca slowly came around again, her face slowly transitioned from looking towards the ceiling to her father. "Have you been wicked, father," she said as she slowly continued on, her head looking again towards the ceiling as she passed.

Then James faced his father and his head slowly lowered, his white, cloudy eyes targeting Paul. "Have we been wicked, father?" James continued to circle as his gaze slowly returned to the ceiling.

Jacob became the next to face Paul. "Do we deserve this, father?"

Paul fell to his knees, covering his face with his hands. When he looked up again, his three children continued to hover and circle, speaking in unison, "Prove me, O LORD, and try me; test my heart and my mind."

Paul shook his head. "Why? Why Psalms? Answer me!"

"Father . . ." James said as he passed,

"Father . . ." Rebecca said as she passed.

"Father . . ." Jacob said as he passed.

"It hurts father," they said together. "Why father? Help father."

Paul keeled over, yelled as loud as he could, "STOP!"

Everything went quiet. Paul looked up, saw they were gone.

"Daddy," whispered a voice.

Paul turned his head and saw his other children. Katy, Julie, Adam, and Bryan were all huddled around Samantha on the couch. "It's okay daddy," Julie said, "I saw it too."

"I told you to take us with you," added Katy.

"I didn't know," lamented Paul from his knees. "If I'd known, I would've taken you all with us."

"It wouldn't have mattered," Bryan said.

"And you didn't know," snapped Samantha. "How could you have?"

"But, now you do," remarked Adam.

"And since you do," continued Bryan, "you can better answer the question."

"What question?" Paul asked.

Samantha laughed. "Surely, you must know."

"Haven't you put it together yet?" Katy asked.

"Put what together?" questioned Paul.

The five laughed in unison.

"He doesn't yet understand," Adam said.

"Perhaps he did not read closely enough," added Julie.

"He read enough," Katy said sharply.

"Perhaps he is simply having a difficult time relating the context," speculated Bryan.

"Perhaps he refuses to focus on the question for fear of what it would mean," Samantha added.

Paul no longer saw the faces of his children. They looked upon him, but he saw evil behind their eyes. "Who are you? What are you?"

"Perhaps he is not ready," Katy said.

"You *are not* my children," Paul snapped. "You're evil."

The five laughed in unison.

"He is definitely not ready," they all said.

"Read for what?" questioned Paul.

The five continued laughing.

"Ready for what?"

The five sat as the couch suddenly caught fire, flame instantly engulfing them all. As their flesh began burning, the laughter halted and screams followed.

"DADDY!" they yelled.

Paul heard his children's voices again; their cries for help. He stood and rushed to their aid, but just as he did, the flame flared up and threw him back against the fireplace.

When he hit the bricks he was back amongst the ashy grounds, surrounded by the burnt foundation of the old house. Grimacing, he reached for his back as the cold night wind stung his skin. His back pain suddenly went away when he saw the shadow standing before him, no more than thirty feet away. "You . . . Why? . . . What are you? . . . Why have you done this to me?"

The shadow stood still.

"Answer me!" Paul yelled, picking up a brick to throw. The brick went right through the shadow, landing a few feet behind it. "Why?" Paul yelled. "Why don't you just kill me and get it over with?"

Paul leaned back, his chest suddenly pounding like it would explode. The shadow came closer. The closer it got, the more Paul's chest pounded. "Why?" Paul asked with what he believed were his last gasps.

The shadow stood over Paul. Once Paul became certain his heart would explode, the shadow bent down, put its hand to Paul's head, then disappeared. Pressure built in Paul's whole body, as if he'd been filled with another being. When Paul felt like he'd just taken his last gasp of air, everything went dark.

CHAPTER SEVEN

Evil Infecting

Sweat beaded from her neck, the sun's light filling her with comfort. Paul stared at her every now and then as they lay out on the grass, her hands running through the tiny blades. She loved it when she caught him gawking at her; even more the joyful sounds of her children playing down by the water. They were safe, she didn't even need to look, not with Paul around. Her gaze remained fixed above, to the clouds slowly dancing their way across the sky. She was in heaven.

Sarah awoke to the sound of birds chirping. She looked up, out the window. The morning fog was nearly gone. If it wasn't for the light crashing down upon her through the window she could have slept all day.

After throwing the covers off and sitting up, her feet touched the carpet, immediately bringing her back to reality. She had forgotten that she slept in the guest house; she had forgotten that her children were no longer with her; she had forgotten that her home was no more. The cold crept back in.

Noticing her bed was empty, she casually went downstairs and straight out the front door. Approaching the ruins, she saw Paul just sitting by the old fireplace. "How long have you been out here?" she asked, stopping about ten feet from him.

Paul didn't respond. He stared blankly out to nothing.

Sarah smiled. "I had a wonderful dream. We were all together again, just over there near the lake. It was perfect. I somehow knew I was dreaming, but I'd forgotten about everything else. It felt so real. Perhaps that was why I didn't want to leave it." Sarah looked at Paul. "Are you dreaming? . . . If you are, I hope you never wake up."

Sarah walked up to Paul, knelt beside him and looked over his face. His eyes were open but he seemed empty, pupils dilated to the point where he barely had any color in his eyes.

"You *are* dreaming, aren't you?" Sarah smiled, cuddled next to her husband. "Stay there, please. It's better there."

Paul breathed in heavily. His mouth opened as if he had not taken a breath for a long time. Letting it out slowly, his exhale continued and got deeper in tone. A lingering moan persisted after it seemed all the air was expelled from his body. Sarah rose to a knee to face her husband. "What was that, my love?" She again looked over Paul's face, looking for anything. Nothing was said.

A persisting silence lasted as she stared deep into his eyes. "Paul," she whispered.

His eyes snapped towards her, his face lagging behind. His dilated pupils quickly returned to normal size, but had a slight, yellow ring around them before the blue. He saw her, he had to, but didn't seem to care. She curled up next to him anyway.

Three days passed. Visitors came and left. No one could stay long, especially with the smell that began festering within the cottage walls. They told Sarah about it, but she didn't care . . . she couldn't even smell it. Each time before someone left they told her how bad they looked, that Paul's skin was turning yellow and she was more pale than they'd ever seen. Paul never spoke a word, nor had he moved from the couch since Sarah plopped his butt down on it. He just stared out the window all day and night, his gaze unbroken even when a guest snapped their fingers right in front of his face. Her favorite part of the day was when the guests left. She could then curl up next to Paul and sleep with her head resting on his shoulder, just like she was now.

"Mommy," she heard a voice whisper as a few of her children ran by the window and played outside. "Mommy, come with us."

Sarah just stared out the window with Paul, listening to the calls she knew weren't real, but unable to get them out of her head. "I see them, Paul," she said, her head resting on his shoulder. "I see them, but I can do nothing for them."

"Come on mommy," they continued to call to her.

"I would rather dream," Sarah said, "at least then it would feel real . . .. Do you not see them, Paul? Do you not hear their calls? . . . You hear them, I know you do. Just keep dreaming, my love . . . it's better that way." Sarah took a deep breath, closed her eyes, and in a matter of moments was fast asleep.

She found herself back on the grass, but she knew something was wrong. Her children laid face down in the lake; Paul laid flat on his back, his rotting body puffed up, dead eyes staring straight to the sky. Nine graves were dug, marked with names of everyone but her.

"No!" Sarah screamed as her eyes opened. Four deep breaths and her heart slowed. "Not my dreams . . ." she whispered, ". . . you can't have that too."

One more deep breath and she looked to Paul. He sat unchanged, other than his flesh looking like it began to rot, and the yellow in his eyes overtaking more and more of the blue. "Are you fighting, Paul?" She rubbed her cheek on his shoulder.

"Mommy," her children whispered again.

"I had the dream again, Paul. It was different this time." She shook her head. "I won't let that be taken too. No . . . I won't . . . I won't." She rubbed her fingertips over his chest. "Paul, do you believe heaven is like our dreams?. . . I think heaven might *be* our dreams. Perhaps when we dream, we're looking at eternity, one of an infinite number of possibilities waiting for us. Maybe, if we can concentrate hard enough on a single dream, we'll never leave it." Sarah sat silent, thinking about her children playing and husband lying out with her on the grass. "If I could die and live in that moment forever I'd do it . . .. I wouldn't even care if it was heaven. It'd be my heaven." Sarah rocked back and forth holding onto Paul's arm, thinking soon she might not even be able to keep her dreams to herself. "Maybe that's all heaven is," she said with a smile. "Maybe . . . maybe . . . maybe . . ."

Three days passed without a visitor.

Sarah remained by Paul's side, her children's voices ringing in her ears. When she touched his white shirt or blue jeans, the stained ashes no longer brushed off. Her breath steamed the cold night air, as did Paul's on the rare occasion he exhaled. She heard a pounding at the door, but didn't move. "Sarah?" the voice called out. "Paul?"

"It's another trick, my love," Sarah whispered in Paul's ear. "No one's there, it's just another trick played by the mind."

"I know you're in there, you two. Sarah . . . Paul . . . people are talking, they're throwing around words like murder. The church removed Paul as head pastor . . .. You guys, open the door! . . . Fine, I'm coming in." The lock turned and the door swung open. "Sarah, Paul, there you two are. My God, Paul, you must be freezing in that dirty t-shirt . . .. Hey! Paul . . . Sarah . . . what's the matter with—oh my God!"

It was Fran from church, standing aghast with her hand over her nose and mouth. "Go away," Sarah said softly.

Fran bent over in front of them, her hands still covering her nose. "Sarah . . . Paul . . . Paul, oh my god, you need to go to the hospital." Fran grabbed Paul's arm, but couldn't budge him. "Paul!" she shouted. "Sarah, look at him! He looks like a corpse! His skin . . . its . . . necrotic . . . it's tearing . . . Sarah, Paul's skin is tearing, can you see this!"

"He's fighting," Sarah whispered.

"Fighting death! My god, and look at you . . . you're so pale, you look starved . . . dehydrated . . . when was the last time you ate or drank anything? Sarah? Sarah, do you hear me?"

Sarah didn't respond.

"Sarah, it's me, Fran," she tried kneeling in front of them. "I told you I'd come back to check up on you. I took a key to make sure I could get in." Fran got to her feet, walked to the side of the couch. "This is insane." She rummaged through her purse, pulled out her cellphone. "I've seen enough. You two need professional help."

"Stop," Paul groaned in a voice that did not sound like his alone.

Fran's thumb hovered over the send button, her face struggling as she tried to hit send. "What's happening to me? Why can't I move?"

Sarah sat up, looked to her husband. Paul's head slowly turned towards Fran, his once blue eyes glowing yellow around a giant black hole.

"Leave," Paul said. "Tell no one, and do not return," his deep and screechy voice echoed and hissed.

Fran dropped her phone and the key to the cottage, then ran through the doorway, not bothering to close it behind her.

Paul turned his head back to the window. Sarah smiled, rested her head back on his shoulder, then closed her eyes.

Morning came and went, then the sun set on another day of Sarah cuddled by Paul's side. She dreamt many times of her family, so much so she convinced herself she could control what she dreamt. She went to heaven whenever she was tired.

Sarah's eyes slowly opened after another dream. She looked to Paul, wondered how a dead man could still breath. She couldn't see him anymore. All she saw was a decomposing body, and every hour or so a little breath escape his mouth.

Sarah struggled to her feet, stood right in front of him. His glowing yellow eyes stared right passed her out the window. She followed his line of sight to the ruins. "Don't fight too hard," she said, turning back to Paul. "Or else you might win." She bent over and gave him a kiss on his rotten lips. "I'll see you soon, my love."

Paul's gaze remained fixed out the window as Sarah pulled away.

Sarah walked out the front door. Only her steaming breath told her how cold it was. The wind blew through the night, but she walked steadfastly to the ruins. As she approached, she came upon some ropes amongst the tarps and shovels left behind from when the debris was cleared from the old home. She grabbed a thin rope and continued on. She came to the remains of the brick fireplace that used to be part of the family room. Climbing the few feet, she secured the rope to the structural beam that still held strong. She tied the other end and wrapped it around her neck. Standing atop the rubble, peering into the window of the guest house, all she could see was the dark form that used to be her husband sitting on the couch, its glowing eyes staring back at her. "You won't take them from me." She looked up to the heavens, dangled one foot over the edge, gazed once more into the guest house. Still, the unmoved glowing eyes were all that stared back at her. She chuckled, then hopped off the bricks with heaven on her mind.

CHAPTER EIGHT

Evil Testing

Paul awoke in complete darkness, his body invisible to his eyes. There was resistance under his feet, but only slight, as if he floated on solid ground.

"Hello," Paul called out, but nothing was returned.

When he took a step forward a ripple formed and shot out from under him. Within the ripple was a small ray of light bright enough for him to see his body, but only for a moment. The ripple carried the light outward in all directions until it faded completely. No matter how far it went, darkness still surrounded him.

"Hello," Paul said again, but like the ripple, not even an echo was returned. "Hello!" he yelled, but still nothing.

Paul walked normally after a few tentative steps, seeing infinity in every direction possible. "Is anyone here?" Paul yelled. "Oh, Lord, my God, I am in need of your mercy. Please shine your light on this desolate place. Show me the way and give me the strength to continue."

An unmeasurable amount of time passed. Countless ripples had shot out and disappeared from his footsteps, none of them getting him closer to anything. It was as if he walked in place. "The Lord is my shepherd; I shall not want . . ." Paul recited again. He had used the Psalm as a marker of time as much as a prayer for strength. After he counted over one-hundred recitals he started losing track of numbers. The marker of time quickly became useless as he had long ago given up trying to know exactly which number he was on. It had to be over a few hundred by now. "He maketh me to lie down in green pastures: he leadeth me beside the still waters. He restoreth my soul: he leadeth me in the paths of righteousness for his names sake. Yea, though I walk through the valley of the shadow of death, I will fear no evil: for thou art with me; thy rod and thy staff they comfort me. Thou preparest a table before me in the presence of mine enemies: thou anointest my head with oil; my cup runneth over. Surely goodness and mercy shall follow me all the days of my life: and I will dwell in the house of the Lord forever."

When Paul looked back, he saw no genesis; when he looked forward, he saw no end.

"The Lord is my shepherd . . ." Paul just kept going, his faith keeping him afloat.

Another unmeasurable amount of time passed with no change.

Paul continued to move on faith alone. Every avenue of thought took him to a paradox. "The Lord is my shepherd . . ." He was not hungry, or thirsty, did not feel anything physically; only mentally he was exhausted, so much so he was convinced he would die. This could not be heaven, but how could *he* be in hell?

Upon finishing another recital of Psalm 23, he noticed ripples traveling towards him. He stopped. All ripples stopped as well. When he took a step forward, the ripples continued, both towards and away from him. He stopped again.

Just then, the dark, liquid-like ground began forming a shape in front of him. Slowly it rose like something was coming through from underneath. The form began rapidly shifting to what looked like different people. The lower half was a solid form, but the upper half formed a torso, arms, and even distinct facial features. The dark, rippling shape did not last long before it switched to another.

"What are you?" Paul asked.

"What would you like me to be?" it asked, its tone deep and terrifying.

"Be what you are!" demanded Paul.

No answer came. The form continued to shift with no apparent reason before solidifying into a dark form that resembled his daughter.

"Rebecca," Paul whispered.

"Ask your questions," it instructed in Rebecca's voice.

"It's not you . . ."

"It is *I*."

Paul took a deep breath. "The shadow," he mumbled. "Where are we?"

"You are with *Me*."

"Why are we here?"

"For you."

"Why me?"

"You were chosen."

"For what?" questioned Paul.

"To be tested."

"Tested? For what? I don't understand." His daughter's image quickly became too much for him. "Who are you?"

"The one who issues the test."

"*WHO* ARE YOU?"

"Who would you like me to be?" it calmly replied. The form again went dark, shifting to different figures.

"Are you Satan?"

The form then shifted to a winged creature. Angelic beauty. Golden hair curling over its shoulders, its whole body shining as it shed the dark, rippling liquid. Its eyes were of fiery gold, outlined in darkness, but somehow looked to comfort and console. It rested on top of the black pillar that formed from the ground on which Paul stood.

Paul took a single step back before stopping himself. "The Lord is my shepherd . . ."

"Paul, we must continue."

"Yea, though I walk through the valley of the shadow of death . . ."

"Is that what you expect?" it hissed. "So be it."

The entire ground lit up in flame. A strong wind put Paul on his back. He looked up in horror at the swirling fire. Up it went like an inverted tornado, of which he was in the middle. Paul sat with his arm shielding his face. The loud roar of fire was deafening—the light blinding—the heat scorching. The fire circled him and his adversary, who sat on its black pillar, as if controlling the wind and flame.

"Is this what you prefer?" it asked over the loud roars of the fire.

The fire shot out in opposite directions. Above him now was darkness. Behind him was a trail of where he had been. Before him was a trail of where he could go. On either side the flame burned atop the black ground like a sea that had just been parted.

"I give you a choice," it continued amongst the sounds of wind and fire. "You can continue wandering around here for eternity; or we can continue our conversation."

Paul's whole body trembled, teeth chattering against each other, arms lacking the strength to push himself to his feet. He could only do one thing. "The Lord is my shepherd . . ."

"Very well."

A blinding light shot out from the winged creature. An explosion followed that extinguished the flame and put out all the light. Paul closed his eyes and was blown a ways back. When he opened them, he was back in the darkness. He could not see himself anymore. His hands touched the ground—a ripple shot out.

Slowly, Paul got to his feet, and continued walking.

"The Lord is my shepherd . . ."

Paul must have recited the Psalm another few hundred times before giving it up. Now he'd walked in silence longer than he had before. He felt eternity, forever walking in place outside of time.

All thought had stopped. Questions only led to contradictions; speculation only led to madness. He was exhausted.

Finally, after so long of struggling in ignorance, moving forward on faith alone, he stopped. Falling to the ground, he was unable to walk any further.

Ripples again flowed in his direction. Picking his head up, he got himself to his knees as the black ground slowly rose. The black liquid shifted forms. Again, the winged creature resulted, but it did not shed the darkness. It spoke from within the liquid. "You are running out of time."

"For what?"

"Your body is almost dead."

"Why do you care?"

"I cannot allow that to happen."

"Why not?"

"Without assistance, the mind cannot live without the body. And we have not yet finished the test."

"I will not take *your* test."

"It is not *my* test. It is my masters."

"You have no master!"

It remained silent a moment, continued to shift form—a wing would melt into the blackness while another formed simultaneously. Its face continuously and unnaturally shifted expressions. "I need to ask you a question," it continued, "but I need you to reach an understanding before I do."

"You are a liar and a giver of misinformation."

"I do not lie."

"You have taken from me, tortured me with the very thing that was taken."

"I took from you; but only as part of the test."

Paul snapped. "I refuse your test! Give me back what you've taken from me! Send me back to my wife and give me back my children!"

"Your wife is dead."

Paul shook his head. "Again, you lie. I want to see her—I want to be sent back! Send me back!"

Paul came to on the couch in the guest cottage. Immediately he keeled over on the ground. He'd felt this before. This time the sensation was much more intense. The room spun and he was nauseous. The pain from moving was overbearing. When he dry heaved his stomach felt like it was coming up. He was just about to pass out when the spinning began to slow, his body calmed, and his mind eased. He looked up, saw his reflection in the glass. His eyes glowed a slight yellow. "Leave me!" he yelled.

"You will die," whispered a voice.

When Paul looked upon his flesh he gasped at his condition. "How long have I . . ." he stopped when he remembered Sarah. "Sarah!" he called out in a weak, raspy voice. Paul picked himself up, but fell back on the couch. "Sarah," he called again, no louder than the first.

His eyes looked to the ruins, saw through the clearing fog someone swinging from the structural crossbeam of the old house. "Sarah," he wailed when he saw her hanging, her neck broken.

Paul struggled to his feet and barreled outside, stumbling all the way to the ruins. As he approached, Sarah became more clear: her lifeless body dangling while discoloration painted her flesh. He grabbed her by the waste, tried to hold her up so she could breath. "No," he cried, "You're alright, you're gonna be okay."

Paul broke down, fell to the ground beneath her, and cried without dropping a single tear.

"I'm sorry, Paul," Sarah's voice whispered in his ear.

When Paul turned to the voice, everything changed. He was back in his fully furnished family room, Sarah no longer hanging from the rope. Alone he knelt on his family room floor, a fire burning beside him in the fireplace. When he looked over his body, his flesh was healthy and his body felt strong.

"Hello Paul."

He broke down when Sarah walked into the kitchen through the archway. "You're not Sarah. You killed her."

"I did not kill *her*, Paul. She chose her end." Paul shook his head as it walked into the family room. "I am no more responsible for your situation than is a hurricane for destroying a city. You can blame me, but you miss the point when you do." Paul looked away, continued shaking his head. "I see we cannot continue like this." It transformed into Paul, looked just as Paul had when he came upon Sarah's hanging body. His flesh was rotten and his yellow eyes had a glow to them. "Is this better? Does this better suit your expectations?" It continued forward, sat on the floor within arms' reach of Paul, right next to the fire. "We must finish the test."

Paul spat its way. "Satan!"

"Name me what you like, I have heard them all before."

"My children?"

"My hand may have dealt the blow, but I can only do what I am meant to do."

"What are you meant to do?"

"Love . . . and issue the test."

"What test?"

"THE test! It is the reason why you exist. It is nothing more than a simple question."

"Then ask it, and let us be done with each other."

"It is not *that* simple. Like I said, before I ask it, you must reach a certain understanding."

"What must I understand?"

"You must understand that my master is a jealous master and only wants to be loved, as I love Him, but I do not have free will. Such is why *you* were created. The test is designed to show whether the love my master craves is present in the subject. It is why I hate you so much. I only do the one thing He expects of you; but where you would be loved, I became the cast out, forever destined to test those of you He finds promising."

"Who is your master?"

"I think you know."

Paul shook his head.

"Yes, Paul, do not run from your revelation, or else we cannot continue. The only way to complete the test is to accept it as it is. You wish to know why the good suffer, I can see the question inside your mind. It is quite simple: the good suffer so they can be tested. They are the only ones worthy of it. The suffering is necessary for the question to be applicable. The test shows whether they can love my master unconditionally. You have seen the outline of the test before, I know you have—you are thinking about it right now."

"But . . . free will . . ."

"Is necessary for choice, and choice is necessary so there can be a test," it explained. "Without free will, the test would have no meaning."

"You . . ."

"I only issue the test. I shed light upon the few souls privileged to undertake it; I bear light upon the subject so my master can make His judgement."

"You enjoy this, don't you."

"I enjoy nothing," it answered. "I perform a task; I interpret behavior; I relay and receive messages and follow orders. My orders entail a bit more freedom than my brothers and sisters."

Paul thought of salvation.

"Do not worry about being reborn," it counseled. "Worry about the test. It is not enough to simply believe my master exists, to have faith that it can bestow upon you happiness and eternal salvation. To be reborn, you must pass the test: You must therefore be perfect, as my master is perfect.   You must love my master unconditionally, as He wishes to be loved."

Paul shook his head.

"Yes, Paul, you had it correct in your last sermon, which is why you were chosen. If nothing else, keep your faith."

Paul keeled over. "How can I?"

It gently placed Its fingers under Paul's chin and raised his head. "I can count on your hand those who've passed the test. However, many have been able to keep their faith. If you can continue trusting whatever it is you hoped my master to be, you will be able to continue living and have that faith rewarded. Those who have maintained their faith and deference have been restored their worldly possessions; they have lived out their lives in relative happiness."

"When they die?" questioned Paul, caring nothing but for his family.

"If one does not pass the test, then death comes just the same. There is a reason why heaven is a lonely place; why my master sits alone."

"Yet you love Him?"

"I do. But what I am is unbounded by the rules that bind you. I can see the answer even now, but I am bounded now to ask you a question . . .. Do you love my master intrinsically, unconditionally, regardless of what is bestowed upon you, whether it be good or evil?"

Paul was broken in mind, body, and spirit. "How can I?"

It nodded. "Your answer is known. People can live without faith, but not after being tested—it is too much for them. Not only have you failed the test, but you have lost your faith. Usually, faith is lost when the subject no longer trusts in their hope. Most hope my master exists but become unable to trust in it. You, however, are certain my master exists, but now wish that it wasn't true. Living for you would now be unbearable."

"Why?" Paul asked. "Why all of this?"

"My master has faith your kind will eventually reach the standard He desires."

After It answered, It bowed its head to the floor. Upon rising, Its face was clear of marks and Its eyes no longer glowed. It looked exactly as Paul did in that moment. Paul felt like he was in the presence of something different.

"I only want my family," Paul said, now unable to see his children's faces, or his wife's.

"You must now, in your final moments, look upon this as a gesture of mercy."

Paul scoffed. "*Mercy* . . .. Mercy would be to have never been born."

"In a moment, you will not be aware that you had been." It leaned over to Paul, raised its arm, extended two fingers and gently placed them on Paul's forehead. It looked through Paul's eyes and into his soul. "Now you will feel no more."

Paul trembled, everything went dark. Then . . ..

"He's got the whooollle world, in His hands; He's got the whole wide world, in His hands; He's got the whooollle world, in His hands; He's got the whole world in His hands . . ."

COMING SOON

Repository for the Unwanted (paranormal / historical-fiction)

A Bridge Between Gods & Man (a sci-fi trilogy)